PRAISE FOR D.D. MIERS & GRACELEY KNOX

"The dawn of a new age of vampire." - **Crafting Geeky Bibliophile**

"*Thirst* is the first in a new series from the writing team of Graceley Knox and D. D. Miers. Whatever they are doing, they are doing it right because *Thirst* had me riveted." - **Tome Tender Book Blog**

"The premise for *Thirst* is so unique... And these aren't just vampires, they are Kresova." - **IB Book Blogging**

"If you haven't read any books by Graceley Knox or D. D. Miers well get busy because you are missing out on two very gifted story weavers!" - **Goodreads Reviewer**

"A CRAZY, WILD, INSANE RIDE THAT KEPT ME ON THE LEDGE" - **Marie's Tempting Reads**

USA TODAY BESTSELLING AUTHORS

MIERS & KNOX

GRAVESTONES
& WICKED BONES

SHADOW CREATURES | BOOK ONE

Edited by: Lorraine Fico White
Cover Design by: Lori Grundy at Cover Reveal Designs

GRAVESTONES
& WICKED BONES

SHADOW CREATURES | BOOK ONE

CHAPTER 1

Ivy

Lila Crane sauntered through the creaky door of Porter's Tavern like a goddamn queen. She stood in the entryway, the blue and red neon "Open" sign reflecting in her lavender eyes. She didn't move, waiting for the sea of bodies to spread in her wake. I wished for once her expectations wouldn't be met. That she'd finally experience disappointment, but a beautiful bitch like her always got what she wanted.

Youthful, beautiful—and a soul blacker than coal.

Her arrival could only mean one thing: his fucking majesty was summoning me again.

Not that Bastian Marquis was actual royalty. Well, technically, the ancient Fae could've been, but I didn't have the slightest idea. It was just the nickname I'd given him. He certainly acted like it, and of course, he'd chosen Lila as his messenger. My severe distaste for the woman seemed to fuel his desire to send her.

Everyone assumed *if* supernaturals existed, they lived in glamorous, mysterious cities like New York or London. But the truth was, hiding out in the least obvious places gave them the freedom to do as they chose. No one cares about what happens to a shitty little town in the middle of the Southern California desert. Especially in *Shelton Sea*, a desert town whose name mocked its total lack of water.

Here, they owned the world. They were each gods—and I an unwilling minion.

Instead of heading straight for me, Lila detoured left toward the back side of the bar. She rarely handled other business when she was sent to summon me. I pitied the idiot who'd been foolish enough to get caught up in Bastian's schemes willingly.

A legendary UFC matchup and cheap beer had packed the regulars into Porter's, every seat in the house taken by the weary, the drunk, or the apathetic. At the edge of the bar sat Lester Simmons and his girlfriend, Winnie; a couple who loved to fight as much as they loved to . . . well . . . you get the idea. They bickered constantly and fought often. Who needed cable TV when those two were around?

Flirt, fight, screw, repeat. Their never-ending routine.

Winnie was in rare form tonight. Her target? A leggy red-headed tourist who'd been unfortunate enough to catch Lester's surly, six-beers-deep gaze. She didn't welcome the attention, but she sure as hell had it.

In my two years at Porter's, I'd learned to tune out the drunken yelling, but it didn't blind me to it. I pulled the tap, filling a scuffed pitcher with pale maple lager, as both women's voices raised over the classic rock from the speakers above. Winnie had a good fifty pounds on the redhead, who'd shrunk away in an attempt to make herself invisible. Fat chance. The Amazonian blonde cornered her against the bar, jabbing a finger into the other woman's chest.

I glanced around for Clive or Porter, the two men whose job it was to intervene on occasions such as these.

Even through the masses, Clive's dusty cinnamon hair stood out. His official position? Designated bouncer. But more times than not, he was too busy trying to get laid to notice—or care. At present, he leaned across the pool table, attempting to demonstrate a pocket shot to his ex. The devil himself could ride down on a flaming steed and still, Clive wouldn't move.

I scanned the crowd, searching for Porter's signature black cowboy hat. At six-foot-four, I'd easily be able to see it above the other, average-sized, humans, but it was nowhere in sight. He must have still been restocking the basement.

Their absence left Violet, Jade, or myself. There was no way in hell I'd let my sisters get involved in any of this crap. As the oldest, it was my job to protect them from the enemies they didn't even know they had, including stupid humans who couldn't hold their liquor.

We were forever changed since *it* happened to us, but it didn't eliminate the humanity within our hearts. It was our greatest strength and our eternal weakness. We each had a unique set of "gifts," as Bastian called them, bestowed upon us, but I remained the strongest. Specifically, thanks to a special present he'd saved only for me. A secret I had yet to divulge to my sisters.

Glass shattered across the bar, and I sighed. Porter didn't mind the arguments. Hell, they were a part of day-to-day business, but he never allowed altercations on fight nights. The cops would undoubtedly get called, and the fire chief would shut us down if we broke capacity rules again.

Neither Porter's wallet, nor my tips, could afford it.

Son-of-a-bitch.

I slammed the pitcher down onto the counter and crossed the bar. We couldn't risk drawing any more attention than we already had, especially from the other supernaturals. If they knew what we were, what Bastian had made us into, they'd be clamoring to get their hands on us.

Half-breed creatures. No longer human but not born into the supernatural world. Made. *Created.*

"Enough." I caught Winnie's calloused fist in my hand, stopping her from bashing the terrified tourist.

3

Any other woman—or man—would have been too intimidated by her massive frame and sheer attitude. Not me. I had the strength of ten men, maybe more, and unmatched speed.

Winnie's glossy, ruby-tinged eyes bugged out as they flashed to her enormous hand locked in mine. "What the hell?"

She tried to pull herself free, but her efforts were in vain. Getting out of my grip, especially when I wanted you there, was an impossibility.

"You know the rules on fight night, Winnie." I kept my tone low. Unlike most of the brawlers in this craptastic town, I didn't like to advertise my abilities.

She made a second attempt to remove my hand, without result. "This little slut's trying to make a move on my man."

Untrue, but you can't argue with stupid.

She jutted her jaw toward the woman cornered and cowering a few feet away. "You expect me to do nothing?"

I took my other hand and turned Winnie toward the door. "Time for you to go."

"LikehellI'mgoin'." The words slurred into one another, and she stepped into my space, a sign she was prepared to take this to the next level.

Too bad for her. I was, too.

"I'm not gonna ask again, *sweetie*." My fingers crunched down onto her knuckles, the pressure just a flex of my wrist from breaking them.

"Shit!" she screamed as she tried to claw her way out of my steely grip.

I met her eyes, and only for a moment, I let the creature inside flash to the surface. As soon as I released my hold on her, she jumped away. Her normally pink face was ashen and sweat-covered.

"What the fuck?" Her eyes widened as she looked me over. The question in her stare: *How had I managed to get one over on her?*

I waited, expecting to go another round, but for once, she surprised me. Winnie stormed off through the crowd, Lester trailing behind her like a groveling dog.

Violet grinned at me from across the bar, and I gave her a wink. Too often, I had to keep my abilities under wraps. When I did release them, which wasn't often, my entire body radiated with a sense of peace.

Our powers simmered within us like a pot of rapidly boiling water, waiting to break free and flow over. I looked to Jade and smiled, only to have my humor instantly fade. Her expression the exact opposite of Vi's—concern laced with tension and fear.

I'd put myself at risk.

Us at risk.

Again.

More than anything in this world, I hated disappointing my sisters. And I would do anything to avoid it, but I have a code I live by, and I don't veer from it. Number one on my list? I don't believe in living in fear. Only in awareness.

Lester and Winnie were drunk off their asses and so were the other patrons. They wouldn't have the slightest recollection of what happened by the time tomorrow morning's hangover set in. Aside from wounded pride, no real harm had been done.

A hand softly tapped my shoulder, and I turned from my sister. The meek redhead who'd been seconds from getting her face pummeled stood and squeezed between two stocky bikers to reach me. "Thank you," she said, her eyes glazed over in some kind of heroic appreciation for what I'd just done.

I hated when this happened. Why did humans always get the wrong idea?

"Don't thank me. I didn't do it for you." I grabbed her jacket off the counter and tossed it into her arms. The leather cuffs smacked her in the face. "Move on."

Her mouth hung slack as she froze in place. Perhaps she expected to hear an apology for my abrasive behavior—which wasn't going to happen. I stood there, returning her stare with one of my own, until she shook her head and left.

I'm not a dick. *Honestly.* But I don't have time to be anyone's hero. My job is to save my sisters from this life. No more. No less.

So far, I'd been able to buy Jade and Violet time. Time to live freely without being held to Bastian's constant call. I'd been doing his dirty work for the last five years, but I know their time is wearing thin. Soon, he'll summon them, just as he did me. Not something I wanted for them, or would allow to happen.

As Bastian returned to my thoughts, so did Lila. She slid into the newly vacant seat in front of me. A humorous smile lingered on her lips from watching my altercation.

"Ivy." She lifted Lester's abandoned glass of clear liquid and tossed it back with ease. "Bastian wishes to see you."

"Of course he does."

Bastian, my supernatural sovereign, and the ever-constant pain in my ass, had a penchant for choosing the worst times to call on me. Fight nights were the only time I made any real money. Unlike some people, I needed to work.

"He does know I can't just leave at the drop of a hat, right?"

She raised her eyebrows, giving me a look which said, *"Are we really arguing about this again?"*

Sometimes it was months, others weeks, but his relentless call came no matter what. The pattern, always the same. Show up at the most inconvenient time, demand my presence with no explanation, and expect unquestioning obedience. I wanted to argue. To say no and screw you, but no wasn't an option.

Stubborn as I may be, even I had to accept the immovable nature of his majesty's rules.

I wiped the sticky remnants of a margarita from the counter. "I'll be there when my shift ends."

"The car's waiting outside." She threw down a twenty and stood. "You've got five minutes."

I watched her disappear through the crowd like a ghost shifting through the mist. As quickly as she'd arrived, she'd vanished.

I spun around and faced the liquor just as Porter sidled up beside me. "You all right?"

"Yeah." I smiled and leaned against the counter. "It's time again."

"Damn, I hoped you'd get a longer break."

"Me, too."

Porter knew our circumstances. He'd always protected us, helped us, but there were limits to how far his generosity could go. He'd offered us jobs, a small rental house, and a car. Even more, he offered us security. Something we'd never had. But he also knew when Bastian came calling, you had no choice but to answer.

As far as I understood, Bastian was the top of the supernaturals, at least for our area. Who knew where he stood in the larger scheme of things. Of course I didn't care. I wasn't interested in getting to know any more of these assholes than I had to.

"You'd better get to it then. He doesn't like to wait." Porter ushered me off, and I slipped into the back office to grab my keys and wallet.

On the way, I stopped in the hallway, my gaze captured by the orange-tinged profile reflected in the mirror. Bastian's experiment had left me the same as before—and yet completely altered. I placed my palms flat against the glass and studied the woman staring back at me. I looked harmless enough but, as they say, looks can be deceiving.

She—*it*—stirred in there. Somewhere deep inside of me.

I continued to regard my face, searching for the creature I'd become. The creature Bastian had made me. He tried often to soften my feelings and turn my hatred of this new world into acceptance, but I couldn't be swayed. In my mind, none of the supernaturals were innocent. Their entire world was responsible for our predicament. They robbed my sisters and me of a future. Of normal lives. Relationships. Children.

Humans were the puppets. The pets of the otherworld. Bastian kept waiting for me to see and accept it, but I couldn't. No matter how long ago we'd lost our humanity, I'd never side with these creatures. Even if it cost me my life.

CHAPTER 2

Ivy

I've never been a patient woman, so waiting for Bastian to grace me with his presence irritated the hell out of me. The Fae were so damn arrogant. Wasting my time like I didn't have better shit to do. The two sets of naked tits staring me in the face didn't help my mood either. Bastian always had naked women here. This pair were new, so he must've tired of his most recent ones since my last visit.

Technically, they had "clothes" on. Although I'm not sure I could call white, see-through gauze sheets clothing. They were more like a thin cloud of air versus actual material. None of them served any real purpose. They were more of a decoration than anything else.

Sometimes I think Bastian assumed seeing sexuality would cause me to feel sexual and, in turn, want sex. More specifically, want sex from him. Since the day my servitude began, he'd offered me an out. Be his, and my sisters and I would want for nothing. I wouldn't allow it.

if I had anything to say about it, no one would ever own me—or us —willingly. Although, I couldn't lie. In the beginning, when I'd been young and naïve, I considered his offer, and I almost accepted. Bastian was exceptionally good-looking. Sexy dirty-blond hair, well-built, and ultra-seductive. But I didn't know anything about him, nor was I sure I wanted to.

How could I ever sleep with the man who created this mess? Who was at least *mostly* responsible for the current predicament my sisters and I were in?

The other half of that equation sat across from me.

Lila.

I never called her Mom—at least not to her face. She didn't deserve the title. She wasn't anything like what a mother should be. Not a single nurturing bone in her dark soul. A soul selfish enough to sell out its own daughters to gain immortality.

She tended to her cuticles as though she hadn't a care in the world. As if the eldest of the daughters she had betrayed wasn't sitting across from her, staring daggers. She tucked back a loose tendril of hair and sighed.

I hated how similar we appeared, my deep black locks and high cheekbones reflecting right back at me on the face of a woman I couldn't stand.

"What?" she snapped.

I must've lost track of how long I'd been glaring at her. She sat back and dropped her hand into her lap.

"What, Ivy?"

I hadn't meant for her to catch me. Why *was* I staring? It was the weak spot inside of me that still hoped she would change. Not for me—for my sisters' sake. Protect them, save them.

But who the hell was I kidding? I've taken care of my sisters since I was fourteen. It's always been the three of us against everything. Even against *her*. Hoping Lila would change was like hoping a starved cheetah wouldn't devour a zebra resting in its den.

"Nothing," I said.

"Clearly you have something you'd like to say, so just spit it out."

"I doubt you *really* want to hear it."

She crossed her arms. "Childish as always."

"What can I say? I learned from the best."

Her sparkling lilac eyes burned into mine, all the unspoken things we wanted to say to each other simmering just below the surface.

Bastian appeared just in time to end our silent standoff. In this light, he almost looked human, his hair smoothed back from his face, the edges hitting his shoulders. A crisp, white dress shirt, black slacks, and crimson loafers covered his tall, slender frame. Bastian was coldly attractive, in a way that would fool most humans, but I saw the true nature of his deception. Bastian was like a beautiful, aged painting–flawless from a distance, the image of perfection but up close, cracking apart.

"Ivy." He walked around the sofa and took my hand, gently placing his lips to my flesh. "It's always a pleasure when our paths cross."

He always did this. Pretended I had somehow come to him of my own volition. Wishful thinking on his part.

"Bastian."

He grabbed a glass of red wine and sat on the long, elegant, Victorian sofa. Bastian's home was an odd mix of the old and modern world. Sumptuous and decadent, yet oddly hostile.

He reached a hand out toward the space beside him. "Sit."

Just as I hit the cushion, a woman brought a plate filled with all the delicacies I always loved. Every favorite treat I couldn't resist.

When it comes to the Fae, it's best to never accept anything they give you. Especially if it seems free. Everything comes with a price. Since Bastian already owned me, there was no point in holding back. I dove into the chocolate truffles, popping one slowly into my mouth. The divine flavor seduced my taste buds, rich dark cocoa with hints of citrus. My sisters and I don't have a lot of money. We get by—but barely. We didn't have money for chocolates or fancy clothes or expensive drinks. So, I took my luxuries where and when I could

He watched me savor the small orb with an interest that set off my guard. He'd made no secret of his desire for me. In fact, he often brought it up. But owning me and having me were two very different things. As much as he could control me in most ways, there were limits to this arrangement.

"What am I doing here?"

Bastian turned to Lila and the living statues. "Ladies, if you'll excuse us."

It was the first time I'd seen him treat his half-naked companions as people and not objects. The act was oddly disconcerting.

When they left, he leaned in close. "I am in need of your . . . *special* gift."

I swallowed a rush of anxious energy. He'd never asked me to use those areas of my powers, and yet, all the while, I'd been anticipating this moment. My debts before this had been standard. He'd used my unnatural strength and stealth but never the part I keep hidden from my sisters.

"There is a gentleman in possession of something I desire." He handed me a photo. "His name is Dante."

My eyes slowly swept over the man in the image. Even on paper, there was no missing the intimidating, commanding presence he exuded. My stomach churned with something I'd thought long gone. Was it desire in me? *Oh bloody hell, Ivy.* I had to shut this down quickly. Dark, powerful men only wanted two things from me: My body or my abilities. I learned that the hard way, and I sure as hell wouldn't fall for another one. I didn't need a man in my life; I mean, why else do women have vibrators?

"What is he?"

Bastian sat forward and snatched the photo from my hands. "It's not your concern."

There was something in his gaze. Irritation? Jealousy? I brushed it off. "What makes you think I can get anything from him?"

Bastian's eyes flowed over my body, tracing arches over the exposed tops of my breasts in my leather vest. "You're exquisite."

"So that's it? You think I'm hot enough for him?"

Bastian smiled. "You've no idea of your unique gifts, Ivy. There is so much more to you."

I looked over the picture again. "What exactly do I have to do?"

The smile playing on his lips unnerved me. "Obtain a vial of his blood."

"You want me to bring you a vial of some guy's blood? You do know how creepy your request sounds, right?"

"He is not just 'some guy' as you say. The task will prove difficult."

I sat back. "So send a vampire, or better yet go get into a fight with him, I'm sure you're good enough to get a single punch across."

"I need it directly from the source and returned immediately. "

"The source?"

"Yes, a very specific source, and there is only one precise way to acquire it."

A million questions popped in my head, but I only asked the most pertinent to my situation. "Why send me?"

"My instincts tell me you may be the only person to get close enough."

Close enough. There was no mistaking the implication. He expected me to act as a hooker. Yeah right.

"No way. I told you, there are some parts of me not for sale." I started to rise from my chair when his hand softly landed on mine. The move was gentle, but his command was clear. Sit.

He moved forward, placing his glass on the table beside him. "I would never have you soiled by such a . . . creature. I simply wish for you to get close enough, bring down his walls, then get what I need."

"And if I am not getting naked for him, how exactly do you think I'll get close enough?"

"A tonic . . ." He raised his thumb and ran it across my bottom lip. "On your lips."

It took me a moment to realize how close he was, and I immediately pushed back to put some distance between us.

"My lips?"

"One kiss, and he won't be able to fight you. It has to be placed directly onto his flesh. You bite his lip, mixing the tonic within his blood, and he'll be out before you know it."

"And why can't you just use one of these naked chicks hanging around here all the time?"

He slowly lifted his finger to his mouth, his tongue tasting me before he sat back. His eyes closed as he savored it.

"I wouldn't be coming to you if any other woman had been able to do so; in fact, I'd prefer you never meet him. But the blood in your heart, so specifically dark, will appeal to him."

The blood Bastian himself put within me.

"Why not just capture him?"

He laughed, as though the idea were ludicrous. "Dante is resistant to normal magic. He needs to be disarmed. So far, I've never been able to get close enough to him. He's quite the beast. I believe you can tame him."

A beast I was about to get way too close to. "What do you want his blood for?"

"Again, not of your concern, my lovely."

The inner alarm inside of me started, it screamed I could never trust Bastian's motives. Did I really want to be a part of making someone else a pawn in Bastian's games?

It doesn't matter because you don't give a shit about anyone else. Remember, Ivy? You, Vi, and Jade matter. Nobody else.

"What do I get out of this?"

He placed a hand over his heart in mock pain. "Is the prospect of making me happy not enough for you?"

I knew my next words would be playing with fire, but this was an opportunity, and I'd become quite the opportunist.

"You've already admitted how difficult this has been for you, which says a lot. If you need this so badly, what do I get if I'm successful?"

People don't give the Fae orders. Bastian could command me to do anything now, and I'd have to do it. Well—almost anything. Maybe I was just getting crazier the older I got.

He looked me over thoughtfully as he contemplated my words. "What do you want? A nicer home? A sizable increase in your bank account? I can do any of these things."

"No. None of that."

He exhaled and ran a hand through his hair. "Then what would make you happy?"

He already knew the answer to this, yet he was going to make me say it. "Freedom. I don't want to owe you anymore. I want my sisters and me to be free. Free to live our lives as we choose, without any of this."

"No."

He didn't even hesitate in his answer.

"No?" I could feel the blood rising to my cheeks. Of course, he'd make me ask, only to decline me. I knew it was impossible; yet, I still had let some teeny part of optimism inside of me have hope.

Girls like me didn't have time for emotions like hope.

"Then, no. I won't do it." I shot up off the sofa, an attempt to stop the adrenaline-fueled shaking from taking over.

Bastian's voice trailed after me, but I ignored him and kept going. I'd never disobeyed him before, and a small part of me was terrified of the consequences of doing so. Sure, I put up a fight most of the time, but I'd never said no and left.

Apparently, my rational mind was losing to the crazy side.

I'd almost reached the foyer when a shrieking noise cut through my ears, sharp and horrid. Debilitating pain spread into every ounce of my flesh, and I dropped to my knees, immobilized. Even when I knew it was coming, I couldn't prepare myself. Bastian's magical leash reminded me of those electrical dog collars. One step too far and I'd get a shock.

There was only one way to make it stop. Obey. Submit. Give in.

But I'm more stubborn than a donkey, so I held out for as long as I could. My invisible screw you. When my pride finally gave way to logic, I surrendered to Bastian's will. Immediately, the pain ebbed.

I collapsed to my knees, panting as sweat spilled down my face. Thirty seconds passed before two high-heeled shoes appeared on the tiled floor in front of me. I raised my chin to see Marla, Bastian's assistant, smiling at me, her pupils cat-like. She held a towel in her hand.

"Oh, Ivy. How many times do you have to test him?" She dabbed my forehead with a warm towel and handed me a bottle of water.

I took a slow swig and smiled. "I guess I'm just not a fast learner."

Unlike most of the supes I'd encountered, Marla was kind. She never treated me cruelly or like a pawn.

"You're smarter than this."

I laughed. "Apparently not."

"There is no way around his magic, Ivy. You're just going to have to work something out with the boss. You can't keep doing this." She bit down on her lip. "You're not the only one who gets hurt."

Guilt burned a hole in my belly. "I know."

If I didn't know a similar pain was being visited on my sisters, even from miles away, I'd probably disobey Bastian more often. But, thanks to our psychic connection courtesy of genetics and Bastian's magic, I was aware of their suffering.

I took a moment to clean myself up before I returned to Bastian. I'd never seen him directly after one of these spells. A gray pallor had consumed his skin, and dark circles formed under his eyes as a light sheen of sweat spread over his brow. He sat on a sumptuous armchair, smirking, his overall attitude belying the fact he was obviously affected by this, too. I never considered these episodes had an adverse effect on him, too. I didn't exactly feel sympathetic to his pain, but I acknowledged it.

"I'll make you another offer." He rose from the chair and came toward me, until we were barely a foot apart.

"There's nothing else you could offer me, Bastian."

"Gravestones and wicked bones, Ivy."

"What?"

"You had to die, return to the grave, so to speak, in order to rise better, stronger with the wicked magic now flowing through your bones."

"What does that have to do with anything?"

He stepped closer, "I didn't do this to harm you, love. It's a gift. You can't seem to accept that."

"A gift that puts my sister and I into indentured servitude for eternity."

He stared at me a long moment, then spoke. "Do this, and I'll free your sisters from my call."

His words stopped me. "You will?"

"Terms and conditions will apply, of course."

He didn't have to negotiate, so I knew if he were to offer something so great, his request in return would be just as large.

"Yes . . . but in exchange, you will remain—forever. You won't ask to be released again, and . . ." His voice trailed off.

"And?"

"And you will allow me a chance to have you."

"I told you, I'm not a whor—"

He tugged on my waist to silence me. "You will allow me to attempt to seduce you."

"Right now?"

"No." He raised a hand and traced the side of my jaw. "Another time, when the mood is right."

From the earliest moments I could remember, my life had been filled with unwinnable circumstances. First our mother abandoning us, and then her betrayal. This was just another to add to the ever-growing list. Maybe it was time to accept the inevitable. If I gave myself up to save my sisters, to give them a chance at happiness, then it was worth it. No matter the cost to me. Right? Besides, Bastian said "an attempt," which meant I could still refuse him . . . hopefully.

He grabbed my chin with his free hand and forced my eyes to meet his. "But remember this, Ivy. This agreement is not to be taken lightly. Choose this, and you will be bound by it. There is no going back. No undoing." He waited patiently as I thought over his offer. "Do we have a deal?"

My sisters' faces flashed in my mind, and I knew my decision was made before I even had a chance to give it a second thought. I'd survived this long, what was forever?

"We do."

Gravel scuffed beneath my shoes as I trudged up to the front door of our basement apartment. Although I'd shared this place with my sisters since Jade was in middle school, it had never really felt like home. Worn paint chipped along the door frame and too many cracks lined the walls. It wasn't anything close to a five-star hotel, but it was *ours*.

I'd wasted the last few hours sitting in the parking lot at a 7-Eleven, contemplating my task. The compact painite red-diamond switchblade Bastian had given me twisted and swirled between my fingers, as countless thoughts swarmed my mind. There was something oddly beautiful about it. The way the colors blended and swirled made it appear as though the metal was constantly moving and shifting.

Bastian wouldn't tell me much. Except it was made from some of the rarest metals and gemstones on earth and the only way I'd be able to collect my trophy. Dante's blood couldn't be retrieved with any ordinary blade. I wasn't sure if Bastian was playing with me; however, as a rule, I didn't refuse free weapons.

By the time I got home, I hoped my sisters would be in bed, and I'd be able to avoid any unpleasant conversations. I dreaded explaining myself to them. Vi, and especially Jade, were too smart—smart enough to worry through all my protests.

The living room lamp glowed like a lighthouse against the dark ocean. No chance of getting out of the talk, and no more time to delay. I had fewer than two hours to get to the airport, and I needed to pack and get my ass through TSA. Bastian's protective magic would only be temporary for allowing me to leave Shelton Sea, and I had to make the most of it.

I jiggled my key in the old, sticky lock. By the time I pushed the door open, Jade was already rushing to greet me.

Her arms flew around me in a tender hug, made all the more stifling by the sticky heat of the air.

"What took so long?" Violet asked from her spot on the sofa. She was sprawled out on the shabby cushions with bits of stuffing pulling free from the arms. Just like when we were kids, one leg dangled over the back, as if she was daring a monster living in the gap underneath to grab her.

"Bastian." I squeezed Jade tightly one last time before I stepped away and retreated to the fridge. The rattling of our AC had gotten louder since last night. "I'm fine. Honest." I snatched a beer out and popped the cap.

Jade hopped onto the counter and tightened her arms around herself. "You're never gone this long."

"Did he hurt you?" Violet demanded from the living room.

The girls never spent much time with Bastian, thanks to our deal. He'd become a mysterious, foreboding figure in their lives. All they knew was he made me sad, distracted, angry, and, on the rare occasion, injured. Naturally, they hated the man.

"Everything is fine," I shot Jade the most genuine smile I could manage. Drops of sweat slipped down my blouse, and I placed the cool bottle against my skin. "How come the air's not on? It's hot as hellfire in here."

"It *is* on," Violet groaned. "You've been hanging out in the lap of luxury too long, you forget how the commoners live."

Jade chewed on her lower lip as she perched on the kitchen counter. "What does he need you for this time?"

"Nothing major." I stared at the peeling linoleum. The cool beer in my palm offered a small reprieve from the sweltering heat. "A simple pick-up. You'll barely notice I'm gone. Maybe a couple of days at the most."

"You're leaving town?"

"A couple days?"

My sisters shouted their objections simultaneously, and Vi jumped up from the sofa, folding her arms across her chest.

"But you can't go past the borders. Not without . . . *it* happening," Jade said, her eyes widening with worry.

"I can," I assured her. "Bastian's taking care of it. Trust me, I'm gonna be okay."

The switchblade in my pocket dug into my hip, a silent reminder of the dangerous task ahead. The enchantment placed upon it would eliminate any chance of airport security picking it up, but the inclination to conceal it remained.

"I just hate this," Jade said, her eyes welling up with tears. "You know you don't have to do this alone. I'm old enough now. We can deal with Bastian."

I slammed the bottle down on the counter. "No. I've told you a thousand times, and I'll tell you a thousand more. This is my responsibility. I'm not dragging you two into it."

"You can't protect us forever," Jade said. "Someday, you're going to wish you'd let us help you."

Violet slid onto the counter to comfort our baby sister. "What about when you run into somebody stronger than you? Someone more powerful? Someone with dark magic?"

I laughed. If they only knew what stirred within me, their doubts would be pacified.

"That's not going to happen."

"How can you be so sure?" Jade asked.

"Because I'm bigger, badder, and meaner than anything else out there." And if anyone messes with me, they're going to have hell to pay —literally.

CHAPTER 3

DANTE

Another day, another blood-soaked dollar.

Chatter and smoke filled the brightly illuminated casino. A muggy, unpleasant film coated my expensive aviators in a filthy residue, but I didn't remove them. The sunglasses were a vain attempt to conceal my identity. Not like I could. A man with my kind of power can't remain hidden for long.

I lifted my glass and tossed back the rich amber liquid. I winced as it burned a trail of fire down my throat. The liquor tasted harsher than its name alluded: whisper. Like a fly to a hot summer's picnic, a pretty young thing wearing a black mini and low-cut top approached my empty glass.

"What can I get ya', sugar?" she asked.

"Macallan, neat. And make it a double."

"Sure thing." She offered me a more-than-friendly smile and sauntered off, swaying her hips for my pleasure.

Of all the things that pissed me off most about my legacy, and there were plenty, my ability to drink endlessly without so much as a buzz secured a spot at the top of the list. Human grain alcohol lacked the strength to give me a little push. If I wanted to experience any effects I had to seek out Faewine, which could only be obtained in under-the-radar bars. Unfortunately, due to recent events, I wasn't welcome at most of those dives.

Some might call me a vigilante. In reality, I do the dirty work for various shady people and organizations, both human and not. My last contract was a total shit-show, and it had cost me years of reputation-building. A human—one of those wealthy, upper-class Wall Street types —needed his boss out of the picture in order to move up the ranks. My moral compass doesn't always point true north, but there are some evils I cannot sit back and ignore. When I discovered his boss was the owner and operator of a huge sex trafficking ring, he became fair game.

Never kill without doing your due diligence.

In the process of destroying the asshole, I'd broken an unspoken code and exposed his Fae daughter-in-law. In this world, you never show your cards. Once the Light Court got wind of it, my hard-earned status took a turn. Now I'm persona non grata.

Here I am, forced to endure the endless chatter and stench of this casino. It didn't smell bad per se, but my keen senses couldn't ignore the thick odor of sweaty flesh and desperation. I pushed a blue chip across the roulette table with the tip of my index finger, eyeing the almost depleted stack. With every rotation of the yellow marble, my money—as soaked in blood as my hands—vanished before me.

The perky waitress returned, setting my drink atop a crisp white napkin. Squares of ice clinked against the glass as I brought it to my lips and inhaled. At least they got the double part right. I sipped slowly and pushed my chips to a spot on the board. As the marble loosened onto the wheel, a ruckus erupted to my right. My senses heightened, and a command called upon my demon to be on alert.

In the center of the hysterics stood Jacoby Peters. The squirrely piece-of-shit was Samil's errand boy. And if he was *here*, it meant Samil had found me.

I wasn't in the mood for his bullshit. I returned my focus to the table, flipping my collar in an attempt to conceal myself from those beady, empty blots of ink. Futile, of course. Jacoby strode toward me with his long, unnatural gait—a trademark of the darker Fae society. His tiny head bobbed with each step.

"Well, well. It's my ol' pal, Danny Argyris." He leaned against the roulette table, cigar in one hand and a Mai Tai in the other.

I could never respect a man, immortal or not, who chose synthetic sugar over an aged liquor.

"What do you want, Jacoby?"

He took a puff of the cigar, filling up his fat, greasy cheeks and blowing a half-assed ring from his lips. I smirked. The Fae had no clue how ridiculous he looked.

He scratched his slicked-back hair and fixed his beady, lifeless eyes on me. It was like staring into the depths of a great white shark and finding nothing but bleak emptiness.

"Boss ain't happy. If the big man ain't happy, ain't none of us happy. If ain't none of us happy, well . . . I think you get the picture."

"I don't work for him. Not anymore." I took a sip and stared straight ahead.

Our croupier pretended not to notice the disruption, continuing to collect bets and spinning the roulette wheel.

Jacoby sucked in a breath and smacked his lips together, creating a resounding pop. "No, no, now, see where you've gone wrong . . . Danny. You don't quit working for Samil. Not till Samil says you quit. He ain't too pleased with what happened in Reno. Far as he sees it, you still have a job to do."

I clenched my fists. He knew how much I hated it when he called me Danny.

Old rage and my savage monster within rushed to the surface. Samil's idiots never knew when to keep their mouths shut. All of Vegas didn't need to know the business dealings of their most esteemed senator. Samil wasn't the name he went by in the mortal world. But you leave enough breadcrumbs and someone will find their way.

"As I said, I don't work for Samil and I'm not running" I paused, choosing my next words carefully, "*false relics* . . . across the border. If he's got a problem, he can come see me himself."

My desire for discretion had nothing to do with protecting Samil and more to do with my own interests. Last I'd heard, Samil was looking for my replacement. Someone who'd be willing to transport his slaves across the border, through Tucson and on to Reno. I don't work with animals of such nature. Heartless dicks who traded in human flesh. Samil was the king of heartless. He made humans into prisoners, forcing them to run all of his illegal business and other bullshit. Not my game.

So, I'd said no and we parted ways. Apparently, our amicable business dissolution wasn't so harmonious.

Jacoby laughed and slammed his stubby hand onto the roulette table. The move sent chips bouncing as he doubled over. "You have no clue what's really going on, do you?"

I had *every* idea, but I wasn't about to broadcast it.

"Find someone else."

He crossed his sausage arms over his protruding belly. "Find someone else? Are you outta your bloody mind, mate?"

I gripped the scotch glass a little too tight. Small cracks like spider webs formed on its smooth surface.

"You need to get your ass back in line before things get nasty." Jacoby lifted the tail of his jacket only slightly—just enough to allow the light to bounce off the curved blade at his waist. It was more than your average sharp knife: it was a branding device. Infused with the magic of the wielder, whoever had the misfortune of being sliced by the fine blade would forever be in servitude to its owner. Highly illegal in the Fae community and extremely rare. How the hell does this dickbag have one?

"I know what you're thinking," Jacoby said.

"Do you?"

He snickered, stepped closer, and lowered his voice so only I could hear. "You think you can outrun me, boy? You think you can keep on hiding from the boss? We're everywhere. Watching your every move."

He nudged his bladed hip toward me. "I'm not the only one with one of these sexy-ass pieces, I can assure you. So, go on. Try to run. I like a good chase. But just know, my slaves eat shit and sleep with their hands tied above their heads. Every. Single. Night."

His breath reminded me of a stale cheesesteak with onions.

"Get. Back."

Before I realized it, the tumbler of scotch and its contents shattered across the roulette table and onto the floor. Shards of glass flew across the aisle to the next station and landed on some poor drunken sod. The tattoos inscribed along my chest and back flamed to life, demanding retribution. Sacrifice. I needed to calm down before I lost control and some innocent bystander paid the price.

Jacoby's eyes widened, and he stepped back. His threatening pose from only a moment ago long gone, like my double scotch on the rocks. With his hands raised, he backed away and blended once again into the sea of humans and shadow creatures.

The waitress from earlier rushed toward me, a white towel outstretched in her hands. "Are you all right?"

She wrapped the cloth around the nonexistent wound, cradling my palm in hers. What she didn't realize was it hadn't broken my skin. Couldn't break my skin. I kept my fist closed and the towel mostly obscured from view to secure the illusion. Crystal-blue eyes gazed into mine as a sultry smile lifted one side of her lips. I knew what she wanted. I could have her in my room and naked in less than ten minutes.

"I've got this, sweetheart. You run along now."

She didn't. Instead, she scooted closer. "It's no bother, really. I have first responder training."

Humans are naturally drawn to the supernatural. Something to do with their genetic makeup and instincts. Place a demon in front of a human and they can't help but throw themselves at it. Right now, this sweet little blonde looked as ripe as a summer peach.

She watched the desire rise in my eyes, setting my fire-like embers to life. Her breath hitched. and she placed her palm on my chest.

I looked down at the foreign hand as it shook slightly. Underneath her desire, she was nervous. Uneasy. I reached out and wrapped my hand around her wrist. Her soul opened to my magic as tiny jolts of thoughts and emotions surged forward. I couldn't get a clear readout on the girl, but I knew one thing—she was desperate. And who better to ploy than a wealthy man who has had one too many drinks over the course of a few games.

I pulled out my wallet and removed a wad of cash. "Take it."

"What are you—"

I grabbed her jaw in my hand. "You're better than this. Better than serving yourself, your dignity, to the highest bidder." I stuffed the cash into her hand. "Now get the hell out of here." I gently shoved her several feet from me.

She hesitated but thought better of it and turned to go, tucking the money into her bra on her way.

Damn humans; they'd sell their souls—or more—for a solution to mortal problems. They had no idea how much it was truly worth.

I removed the unsoiled towel and tossed it onto the nearest trash. Before I could drift into the new Scotch placed before me and self-deprecation, my eyes fell on the most exquisite beauty I had ever seen.

She walked down the center aisle of blackjack tables and baccarat to the whirring slot machines. Her simple clothes couldn't hide how remarkable she was. I could taste it in the air. It surrounded her. An energy, pulsing with a heartbeat. Strong and fierce.

Silky, onyx hair begged to be touched. I wanted to run my hands through it as she lay naked in my bed. Her clothes, although casual, allowed me to admire the curves of her feminine body. She was gorgeous. No, damnit. She was something else entirely, and I didn't have a single word to describe it.

Her dark eyes found mine, and for an instant, a charge ripped through me, turning the markings along my skin to lava. I'd wanted women before, immortal or human, but not like this. It pulled me to her. An invisible magnet.

The spell broke as she looked away, taking a seat at one of the glossy, LED-lit slot machines. Thirty seconds in her presence, and I was mental.

An alarm fired off in the back of my mind, warning me to be cautious. After 200 years, there were few things in this world surprised me anymore. When I found something *did*, I couldn't just walk away.

CHAPTER 4

Ivy

After the long, tedious day, my body hummed with anxious energy, like a kid on Christmas Eve, eagerly awaiting the moment when my presents would be revealed. The prolonged absence of freedom had clearly begun to mess with my head.

I'd rehearsed the plan a few times since I'd left Shelton, but now, faced with the real thing, the real man, everything went out the window. There was absolutely no mistaking him. He sat at an empty roulette table, his short dark hair tipping over the sunglasses he wore.

Bastian didn't let me bring the picture, but he didn't need to. I'd been studying every line and shadow of Dante's face behind closed eyes for hours. I could pick the man out of a crowd of hundreds—maybe thousands. As if my thoughts had drawn his attention, he slowly turned and scanned the casino. His gaze shifted past me at first, then stopped and froze. For only seconds, there was just the two of us. Even through the glasses, his piercing eyes held me captive.

For fuck's sake. Keep it together, Ivy.

I played it cool, mindlessly toying with the slot machine while keeping him in my periphery. I was sure he wouldn't be going anywhere anytime soon, but just in case, I didn't want to lose him after getting so lucky.

Drink in hand, he rose to his full height. I grabbed my purse off the top of the machine, preparing to follow in case he strayed too far.

Except he wasn't *going* anywhere—*he was coming*.

Toward me.

Shit. I focused hard on the brightly colored screen, pretending not to notice the moment of his arrival. He stopped a few feet away from me, but the vigor of his magic reached out, practically kissing my skin. As difficult as it was, I kept my composure, poking idly at the glowing buttons until he cleared his throat.

I turned, letting my eyes steadily drift up his body. Not too slowly, but just enough to let him know he'd struck gold. I leaned onto my elbow, the angle a perfect view down my dress. "Hi."

"Evening." His voice was a low, seductive rumble.

"I didn't hear you walk up."

"Most people don't."

He leaned against the slot machine, caging me in with his body. I still had an open route of escape just behind me. But it certainly didn't feel like it with him this close.

Of all the times I'd casually used my glamour on bar patrons or angry assholes in line at the gas station, I had never once seduced a man I was actually attracted to.

And boy was I. There was no use denying it. Six-foot-four lean muscle, built like an actual god, with a chiseled jaw and just the right amount of I-don't-give-a-fuck stubble. He ought to have looked like a cliché in his worn-out jeans and leather duster, but instead, he looked like a man you never wanted to cross.

"I saw you walk in," he continued. His voice seemed a little rough with disuse, like he wasn't accustomed to talking much. His body dipped toward me. "You know this is no place for a pretty girl to hang out all alone."

"Well, luckily, I've got a knight in shining armor." I smirked up at him. "Or . . . a knight in tattered denim, as the case may be." I twisted the faux-diamond stud on my left ear. "Maybe not a knight at all?"

"Maybe not." He smiled. "But you're not exactly what you seem to be, either. Are you?"

Bastian's warning repeated in the back of my head. *Don't try to fool him; he'll know you're not entirely human. Don't give him a reason to distrust you right off the bat.*

"What do I seem to be?"

He chuckled into his glass. "Besides a sexy hellcat hiding beneath demure clothing?"

Damn. I liked him.

"I'm like you," I told him, frankly. "If you're wondering."

"There's nobody like me."

I let out a soft, enticing laugh. "You might be surprised."

"For once in my life, I'd love to be proven wrong." He glanced at the untouched juice in my hand. "I see you've got a drink already, but will you sit at the bar with me until it's time to buy you another?"

"Sure." I shrugged. "Why not?"

I squared my shoulders and walked toward the bar, conscious I wasn't just trying to come across as a sex object. This was a man who needed to see his own strength reflected back, something truly remarkable, if I wanted to catch him off his guard. I wasn't just prey— but predator, too.

Luckily, that part was true to life.

I slid my hands across the bar top, rubbing the glossy mahogany beneath my fingertips as I sent out the first few tendrils of my influence. As long as he was distracted, he wouldn't suspect me, and my dress was framing my cleavage just right.

I watched carefully for a reaction. Dante wasn't like one of those dullard barflies I could work like a puppet. He was a seasoned veteran. He'd probably been seduced by at least one succubus before, just not one as powerful as me.

At first, he stiffened, but a moment later, he relaxed and eased his elbow onto the bar. I could actually sense it, as if I was rubbing his shoulder and had just worked out a stubborn knot. He was opening up to me.

A hint of guilt crept up, but the heady excitement soon swallowed it. I was seducing a powerful half-blooded gun for hire, and he had no idea what was happening to him. Of course, this was only Step One. Things got significantly more complicated from here. The trick, for now, was to keep it a light touch.

"I'm Ivy, by the way." I reached my hand out toward him and his enormous palm swallowed mine. Rough, warm hands radiating strength and cloaked power.

"Dante."

"So," I swirled the thin black straw in my glass. "What brings a man like you to Reno? Business or pleasure?"

He stiffened just a fraction. Not on the outside, but his energy pulled back and shifted like a wall had risen, only briefly, before falling again.

"A bit of both. What about you?"

"Just visiting."

"I didn't know anyone chose to visit Reno."

I laughed. "You're here."

"Yeah, but not entirely out of choice." He took a sip from his glass and smiled.

"Me neither."

A hostile silence followed my reply, and I immediately realized my mistake. *Shit.*

"I thought you said you were visiting." He didn't move, but his voice held a lethal edge.

I dropped a heavy dose of my influence, letting the tendrils of my magic stroke him with pleasure, serenity, and desire. It was a risky move, but I needed to undo his hostility—and I needed to do it quickly.

"What I mean is, my limited budget dictated Reno. It was close and cheap." I rested my chin on my palm. "If I could have *chosen*, it would have been Hawaii or Paris."

The seconds seemed like hours as they ticked by before his defenses eased again.

Thank. Freaking. God.

We talked for another hour about the city and all the places he'd traveled. Two more drinks down, and I could feel the heat of his gaze on my skin, sense the desire in his eyes. I kept up my carefree, flirtatious appearance, smiling and crossing my legs as I leaned into him every so often.

After my last slip, I remained cautious of my words. It only took a second to destroy all the work I'd already done.

The bartender's voice broke through my thoughts. "Can I get you guys anything else?"

Dante looked to me. "One more?"

I nodded.

"Another for each of us." He turned slowly on his stool until his knees touched mine. His gaze traveled up and down my body before reaching my eyes and staying put. *Unexpected.* Once most men caught sight of my tits, they didn't care to look anywhere else.

Time to move things forward.

"So, does the night end here?" My heart hammered in thunderous repetition, but I kept my poker face. Going up to his room wasn't part of the plan, but neither was the lust burning up my thighs. I could easily apply the tonic-laced lipstick Bastian had given me and finish the first part of this right now, yet here I was, playing with fire.

"Do you want it to?" he asked as he leaned toward me.

Screaming *"Hell No!"* would make me seem too anxious, so I settled for something a little more playful. "Do you?"

His tongue slipped out and rubbed across his bottom lip. "No, I don't."

"Good. Me neither." I rose from the stool and tugged down the edges of my hiked-up dress. "Should we go back to your room?"

He didn't take any further coaxing. He set down his drink, dropped a hundred on the bar, and guided us straight toward the elevators.

I'd just go up for a nightcap . . . and *maybe* a few laps around third base.

Who could blame me? If the word "fuckable" existed in the

dictionary, Dante's picture would be plastered above it. I didn't intend *to* sleep with him, just fool around a bit. Besides, it couldn't hurt to foster the connection before part two of the plan—and nothing fostered it better than physical contact.

Bastian hadn't outright said no, but he made it clear to me I wasn't meant to sleep with Dante. Would he be able to tell?

I didn't know—and I didn't care.

Maybe it was foolish or careless, but there wasn't one thing in my life not currently wrecked. Soon enough, I wouldn't be making a single choice without Bastian's approval, and right now, I'm willing to take the punishment for this. I needed to take my last chance at pure and honest pleasure, and Dante looked like the kind of man who knew *all* about pleasing.

CHAPTER 5

*D*ANTE

This woman might be the death of me—and I don't give a damn.

With every step she took, Ivy's hips swayed—not purposely—but naturally. Full and round, they beckoned to be grabbed. Caressed. Commanded. She could be an assassin for Samil or any number of my growing enemies, but it didn't matter—all that mattered was here and now. Whatever—*whoever* she was—could wait until tomorrow. Right now, I'd be a fool to turn her away.

Strong, beautiful and captivating, I intended to have every inch of this alluring creature. Caution be damned. Besides, I'm Dante Argyris. Crossing me is the path to certain death. If she toyed with me, aside from the way I wanted her to, there'd be hell to pay.

We stepped up to the door of my suite, and I tapped the key card to the metal strip. A green light flashed, and I guided her forward with my palm against her lower back. She crossed the foyer into the main room and walked around, viewing my suite. I wanted to head straight for the bedroom, but my demon's appetite craved something different.

Something else. It took me a second to realize what it was: the buildup. The desire to savor this moment.

"This is incredible." She stood in front of the floor-to-ceiling windows, admiring the expansive city view. "Reno actually looks beautiful from up here."

Everything about this moment was perfection, except for the hand she had wrapped protectively around her waist.

Was she having doubts? No way. I could smell the desire rolling off of her, and yet, her mood seemed to shift. Rife with lust but something else. Something I couldn't quite peg. When she turned back toward me, the uncertainty had vanished and the gorgeous temptress remained.

"Would you like another drink?"

"Sure. Surprise me."

I poured her a glass of rosé and myself another scotch—the way I had ordered it earlier but didn't receive. Neat. No ice.

As I reached her side, Ivy turned and the edges of her full lips crooked into a seductive smile. This close I could smell jasmine and honeysuckle on her flesh.

Shit, I was a lost man.

I offered her the glass of wine, but she narrowed her eyes and smirked as she plucked the scotch from my other hand. She inhaled slow and deep before she brought it to her lips and took a drink.

"That was for me," I said, grinning at her brazen attitude.

"Do *you* like rosé?"

"No."

She tipped the glass and downed the last of my scotch. "Me neither."

The pulse at the nape of her neck beat rhythmically, and I had the strongest desire to cover the sweet spot with my lips. To taste her soft skin and pull a moan from her perfect mouth. She set the tumbler down and moved over to the desk. Her fingers traced a weathered spine as she thumbed through the free books on the shelf.

"You like books?" I asked.

The seductress smiled and clucked her lips, waving a hand from side to side as if to say no-no-no-no. "Who doesn't like books?"

"You'd be surprised. Personally, I love the feel of holding a book in my hands. There's nothing like a great novel to keep you company when you're lonely or in need of an escape."

She tipped her head playfully. "Are you in need of an escape?"

"Aren't we all?"

Her humor faded slightly, and she looked down toward the books again. "There is no escape."

"Of course there is."

"No." She shook her head, "Not really."

What made her feel so trapped?

As if reading my thoughts, she answered my unspoken question. "I have two sisters who depend on me and far too many . . . responsibilities to dwell on things."

"Responsibilities?"

She glanced at me but didn't answer.

It was nice to talk to a woman who seemed truly interested in me and not just my money or power. I wanted to know everything she would tell me, but I also needed to warn her about giving so much about herself so freely.

"You shouldn't speak this openly to strangers."

She laughed. "What am I, six?"

"Being cautious isn't childish. In our world, it's necessary. I have no ill intent toward you, but someone else out there might. 'Trust no one' has been my motto for some time."

"I can see why you need the books."

I grinned, but it was true. A life like mine required sacrifice. My relationships were limited to the very rare and few.

She continued on. "It doesn't matter, anyway. I have someone who watches me. Keeps me from any real harm." Her voice was quiet, far away. Disconnected.

My demon growled protectively. Who was this "someone" she referred to? And why did she say "watches me" not watches *over* me?

What was she hiding?

37

I had every intention of finding out, but she stepped into me, and all rational thought flew out the window.

Her body rested a breath from mine, and I stiffened as a surge of hungry desire raged under my calm exterior. She looked up, her brown eyes studying every angle of my face. Deep, penetrating and surprisingly innocent. I could get lost in their depths and forget all the warning signs.

Hell, I could ignore the end of the world if she touched me right now. It didn't matter where or how, just as long as she did it.

But under all her innocent beauty lurked something dark. I sensed it the second I saw her. Something had a grip on her, blackening her otherwise pure soul. The darkness inside was almost as tempting as the woman it held prisoner. Intoxicating, it reached for me with its inky tendrils. What if those shadows consumed her last ounce of innocence, like my own? I knew what happened when the creature chipped away at the soul. It was a hard and cruel reality check I couldn't let happen to her. I had to protect her. I wasn't sure why or, hell, even how.

"What does this person ask of you in exchange for their protection?"

A shadow crossed her seductive eyes. "Nothing I don't have to give," she answered.

It was only a fraction of a second, but long enough for me to catch a glimpse into her innermost thoughts. Fear. Imprisonment. Captivity. She wasn't being protected so much as she was owned. Someone's property.

A long time ago, another's chains had held me captive in a similar way. I barely knew Ivy, but I didn't want the same for her. She deserved to be free. Free to command her own life. Not used for the vast power storming within her blood. Did she even realize just how much magic she held? I doubted it. If she had, she would've freed herself by now.

"Has anyone ever cared for you without asking something in return?" I asked.

Years of pent-up rage mingled with her silence. She moved back toward the window and I followed. Her eyes cast down to the crystal blue waters of the hotel's pool, distant and cool. A group of humans flailed about, drunk and insolent.

Her pain was old and deep. It surprised me how the darkness hadn't consumed her already; then again, there was something special about her. It probably had to do with all her unharnessed power. How had she not gone full dark and exploded already—a supernova of magic and angst?

I wanted her to come back to me. Gently, I wrapped my hand around her wrist, rubbing my thumb along her flesh to coax her attention.

I waited, giving her all the time she needed to decide what she wanted and didn't want to share.

"That's not the kind of life I have, Dante."

She didn't elaborate, but fury from years of suffering seethed in those few words.

A foreign sensation formed in my chest. Pain, sharp and maddening.

Before I could stop myself, I pulled her close and lifted her chin, so I could look directly into those dark depths.

"You don't have to hurt anymore, darling. I can take it all away."

How, you idiot? How could I make such an empty promise but feel the weight of it in my bones and know full well I would keep it?

"Don't pity me," she said.

"You think this is pity?"

She tried to step away from me, but I caged her in with my body. "I want to help you."

"Help me?" She crossed her arms and her defenses flung right back up. "Do I have 'charity case' written on my forehead?"

"Not at all, but I've been where you are. I can help."

"Oh yeah?" She laughed, but not in humor, "And what's *your* price?"

"Nothing."

"Nothing is free and there is no escape. Not from the cage I'm in." She snatched a tube of lipstick out of her pocket and dabbed it on.

"Ivy . . ."

"No more talking." She grabbed my neck and slammed her lips into mine. A lightning bolt of energy arced and raced through me. I wrapped my arms around her waist and pressed her even further into me and deepened the kiss.

Hungry, I devoured her, inhaling her erotic scent and savoring the warmth she emanated. I blazed a trail of soft kisses down her jaw, to her sweet spot on her neck. She brought my mouth back to hers and bit down. Blood seeped out of my lower lip and my demon roared with molten desire. I grabbed her hips and lifted her off the ground, ready to take this straight to the bedroom.

A banging against the door interrupted my descent of her body.

"Who the hell?"

A nasally voice boomed from the other side.

Jacoby.

The piece-of-shit had just caused me to reach the end of my patience. My lust-fueled desire morphed into rage, and I released Ivy from my arms. That asshole had just ruined one of the best nights I'd had in a while. My demon, unforgiving, prepared to annihilate him and anyone he'd brought.

CHAPTER 6

Ivy

"Get in the bathroom." Dante grabbed my arm, pushing me toward it. "And lock the door."

I twisted out of his grip. "I can take care of myself."

Briefly surprised by my strength, he shook his head. "No doubt. But all the same, you don't want to mess with these assholes."

He tried to shuffle me toward the door again, but I held my ground. "I'm not hiding like some scared child while you play the hero."

"Maybe you've faced down some bad guys, but trust me when I say, you don't know *these* people. If you want to see your sisters again, you'd better get your ass somewhere safe. Now."

"Fine," I grumbled, making my way to the balcony. "Have it your way."

"Where the hell are you—" he asked, but I was already scaling the balcony railing.

"Getting 'my ass' somewhere safe."

"Wait." He called out. "When will I see you again?"

"In your dreams." I winked and dropped out of view.

Bastian had made sure Dante and I stayed on the same side of the building, a few floors apart, which made for a quick and easy exit. I tightened my grip on the wrought iron railing and clambered down the side of the hotel, grateful for the close proximity.

I could hear banging and shouting. Shit. If this whole caper got blown up because of some old enemies of Dante's barging in . . . I guess Bastian couldn't blame me. But it would be a lot of wasted effort on my part.

Grunting, I glanced down long enough to judge the distance between my foot and the next railing. Ugh. Too far. An ordinary girl would probably worry about shattering her ankle, but I just needed to make sure I could keep a firm grip.

I let myself down a little farther. I wasn't quite hanging on by my fingertips, but I was getting too damn close.

If only Jade could see me now.

Just as my grip started to get iffy I flexed my foot and sensed the metal beneath me, solid and reassuring. I slipped my foot behind it, then the other, carefully walking my hands down the thankfully rough surface of the outer wall. When I finally gripped the railing with my hands to steady myself, I let out a sigh of relief.

One floor down, one to go.

The patio door in front of me jiggled.

Well, shit. So much for catching my breath.

I quickly wiped my hands on my dress and grabbed the railing, repeating the same process. The door slid open just as I gripped the bottom of the patio. I took a risk and jumped.

At first, I had the balance I needed, but then my foot slipped. Cursing, I pitched forward and grabbed for the railing with both hands, landing sideways and barely avoiding an embarrassing visit to the emergency room by taking the brunt of the railing to the softest part of my butt.

I rolled onto my own patio with a decidedly unsexy wheeze.

And then I realized I'd left the balcony door locked.

But, when you were outfitted by Bastian Inc., nothing was ever really locked.

I unstrapped my utility kit from my thigh and got to work.

It was almost four in the morning when I'd glanced at the clock again. The prime time for mischief, Violet would say. I'd rather be getting ready to take a steaming bath with fresh ginger shavings, elderberries, and burning sage to clear the negative energy from my space. Instead, I'm about to transform into *her* and rob an insanely hot supernatural with far too much power.

I shuffled and reshuffled the deck of cards housekeeping had helpfully provided. I didn't know if they were supposed to be for gambling practice or something to pass the time while you waited for your expensive hookers to arrive. This place was far out of my wheelhouse. There wasn't a rattling fridge filled with bottles of Bud Light anywhere in sight.

But I had a job to do. The psychic channel I'd opened with Dante told me he was still here and still safe. I sensed his presence, and he wasn't distressed anymore. Hell if I knew how. I didn't really want to know what had happened to the guys who were pounding on his door.

I didn't want to know what would happen to me if I got caught.

But I wasn't going to get caught.

I stared at the lights of the city and the passing cars, small enough to look like toys from up here. There were a lot of people still wide awake, but Dante wasn't one of them. I could feel it.

I glanced over at the clock on the wall. The long hand ticked over . . . once, twice. It was time to quit stalling.

I had to do this.

I took a deep breath and closed my eyes.

At first, I focused on the soft sound of the ticking clock. I let my surroundings melt away, until I could no longer feel the smooth glass of the coffee table under my fingers. I breathed steady and slow. I opened my mind to the awareness of the otherworld lurking beyond the edges of my vision.

I drew a breath in this world and exhaled it in the next.

It was hard to describe exactly how I knew. I'd experienced the shadow form of my succubus once before, but the feeling was unmistakable. The hotel still existed, just as it did in my human world, but it was like a dim reflection of itself.

My succubus allowed me to travel through the world without being noticed, it was all still the same and yet completely different. And it wasn't just in appearance, it was also the objects and people you encountered. Things were different in the shifting world and I had to take care to remember myself. I could easily end up trapped in this space between the living and the dead.

I stopped by the mini-bar on my way out the door. Each bottle was filled with a strange, thick, black liquid I'd never seen before. The labels were written in some unreadable, ancient tongue, which would probably summon an Eldritch horror, a grotesque abomination with unnatural powers.

Sometimes, it's the little things that tip you off.

Slowly, I walked out into the hallway, barefoot. I walked like a ballet dancer, toe-to-heel. Graceful and silent. The elevator took me up two floors, following the glowing trail to Dante's room. It grew stronger the closer I got to him.

And I could hear his voice. He called to me, without even knowing it. His magic called to mine.

Ivy.

On his door, in place of the electronic card reader, there was an old-fashioned brass keyhole. I knew without looking I'd find the matching skeleton key in my pocket.

A gift to myself. The gift Dante had given me, by opening his mind and soul to my influence. His trust.

He gave it too easily.

I slid the key into the lock.

Ivy.

The door opened slowly, but he was already rising to meet me. In this world, he still looked like himself, a dark shadow rising out of the pale, unconscious body on the bed. When I blinked a certain way, I thought I saw the flickering of wings, but I must have imagined it.

His soul was fearsome and beautiful. His deep-set eyes burned like embers. Before I could close the distance between us, his shadow form flashed and appeared inches from me, grabbing my face and pulling it close to his.

Ivy.

I didn't have it in me to feel smug. Yes, he was making this much easier than I thought it would be—but the pull was equally powerful on both sides. I'd never encountered anything like this before. A rush went through my body when he touched me, even the pang of guilt when I looked down at his sleeping form, still resting on the bed, couldn't stop me, couldn't hold me back now.

I needed this, just as much as he did.

The memory of my last conversation with Bastian came to me, unbidden.

"I don't get what you need me for. Can't you just . . . inject him with some crazy purple knockout gas?"

"You don't understand, doll. He's stronger than you realize. Much stronger. Not just in his body, but in his mind and his soul. He'll resist us. The only way to incapacitate him in the physical world is to drain his spirit first. So, see why I need your gift?"

My gift and curse. It seemed like both as Dante's fingers closed around my wrist.

"Ivy." His voice penetrated every defense I had.

I needed to shut him up.

Leaning in and up, I captured his mouth with mine.

Instantly, my body shook with electrified power. The connection between us, stronger than I ever could have imagined. I knew it wasn't just my doing. Even as my influence slowly gained sway over him, tendrils of my powers grabbed onto his strength and tugged it free, sapping it. I still felt galvanized.

I wouldn't be surprised if my hair was standing on end. Goosebumps rose all over my skin, and Dante let out a tortured groan, muffled by my merciless kiss.

If he knew what was happening, it was already too late. I could feel his strength infusing my veins, flowing through my body. He wouldn't be able to fight back, not now.

With each passing moment, I grew stronger. More unstoppable. Even so, his fire engulfed me. Tendrils of smoke rose all around us.

Even as his spirit wavered and collapsed around me, shattering, I could still feel his fire.

I came back to myself in this world, gasping and sweating and shaking.

It was sunrise.

Immediately, I forced myself to stand. I didn't have much time. I had to be quick.

I yanked open the door to the mini-bar, half expecting to find the strange, caustic liquid still there. But, of course, everything was back to normal. I grabbed a diminutive water bottle and chugged it in one go.

Then, it was off to Dante's floor in the real world.

I clutched the switchblade in my pocket, trying to stay grounded in this reality.

As I approached his room, I spotted the housekeeping cart just down the hall. Perfect. This would be even easier than I thought.

"Excuse me," I said softly, approaching the woman. "I'm so sorry; I've been locked out of my room. Is there any way you can let me in?"

I didn't have much energy left, but it was just enough influence to convince this woman not to send me packing to the front desk.

"Do you have your ID on you?" she asked, key card already in hand.

"I can show it to you as soon as you let me in," I told her. "I'm so sorry—thank you so much."

She nodded, breathing in my influence with every inhale. By the time she had his door open, she would've already forgotten about my promise.

"Thank you, thank you," I babbled as she pushed the door open. "You're a lifesaver." I shoved a stack of bills into her hand, just in case.

Heart pounding with adrenaline, I backed against the closed door and stared at the massive bed in front of me. Dante lay prone, one arm dangling off the edge of the mattress, his breathing so shallow, I had to hold my own breath to see the movement.

I advanced toward him slowly. But he didn't stir as I approached. Not a single sound or movement as I pulled out the delicate orange-red blade. I smoothed back the covers and revealed Dante's tattooed chest.

At the center of his breast bone rested three rows of words written in Latin. I ghosted my fingers along the letters. I could've sworn they moved, but I shook off the idea. I hesitated, then sliced across the center of his heavily inked chest, exactly where Bastian had told me to.

Deep red, almost black blood, oozed out of the wound. I set the vial against his flesh letting it seep in, slow like honey.

I glanced to my left and noticed a tray of leftover room service resting on the bedside table. A large jagged steak knife and fork sat atop the empty plate.

Had Bastian lied? Did I really need this particular blade?

I removed the dagger, watching as the wound began to close again and the blood retracting into Dante's flesh. I grabbed the steak knife and reluctantly sliced at Dante's chest.

Nothing happened.

I pushed harder.

Again nothing.

I used all of my strength, taking strikes at his arms and stomach. Still nothing.

So it was true.

What the hell was this man? I'd heard of supernaturals with all sorts of powers and abilities, but the power to not be wounded by a knife? That was a new one. I wanted to stick around and run a few more experiments, perhaps search for answers in his room, but there wasn't time—and in truth, it wasn't any of my business.

With his blood in my possession, I went into the hallway and power-walked to the elevator.

I had held up my end of the deal. Now, it was up to Bastian to uphold his.

I didn't have much time to sleep before my flight home and even less inclination to do so. The effects of siphoning Dante's soul had my succubus flying high, but my body was exhausted, and I needed my strength. Besides, I could take some time to relax. Dante wouldn't rise until long after my flight home. After a few cups of herbal tea and some pacing in my room, I was finally able to lie down in bed and let myself drift off.

My rest wasn't soothing at all. I fell into a fitful sleep, tossing and turning as the truth of my actions weighed on me. I'd been guilty of the very thing I hated Lila for. I betrayed someone who'd trusted me. No, this was even worse. Dante offered to protect me, and I truly believe he wanted to. But what other option did I honestly have? No one screws with Bastian, and my sisters' futures were at risk.

No. Good or bad, I'd made the right choice. *The only choice.*

Hours into my rest, Dante came to me, just like I came to him. But different. He was vengeance, fire, and brimstone. I knew at once we were still in the ethereal plane, but it didn't minimize the wave of fear and guilt. Smoke and hellfire followed his every movement as he stormed toward me. In real life, he was commanding and fierce, but on this plane of existence, he exuded an altogether terrifying savageness.

He grabbed me by the jaw and the embers in his eyes flared with a deep burnt orange.

"I'm not certain of what you've done to me, dark vixen, but know this. I will come for you. No matter where. No matter how far."

He traced a finger along my jaw and tugged me forward until his mouth was flush against my ear.

"Sleep tight, Ivy. I'll see you soon."

CHAPTER 7

DANTE

I blinked and brought the palm of my hand to my forehead. Sliding my fingers down to the bridge of my nose, I pinched and inhaled deeply. Like someone had slammed a blade between my eyes and left it, pain receptors erupted and tingled throughout my body. My vision blurred.

Was I hungover? How could I be? I had a few glasses of the humans' cheap scotch, but I was missing something. A bigger piece to the picture.

What was I forgetting? My mind had a hazy spot. I could remember Jacoby.

Piece of shit Jacoby.

He had nearly knocked the door to my suite off its hinges. The other goons of Samil's trailed behind him equipped with the curved blades of bonding. I hadn't seen more than one etched with the ancient symbols in person, let alone three.

When they finally left . . . what happened when they left? Something, no, someone was missing from my memory.

Ivy.

She refused to hide out and instead took a trapeze act out the patio balcony. Frustrated and furious, I decided to kill whatever liquid I could from the mini-bar. It shouldn't have affected me. *Couldn't* have affected me. Which meant someone had drugged me. But who? And why?

The only people who could've done anything to me were Jacoby—or Ivy. I hated to think the first woman to pique my interest in a hundred years had turned out to be just another ruse in my life.

Bloody hell. That kiss.

Just before Jacoby had ruined my entire night, I tasted pure bliss only to have it— her—disappear moments later. My demon swarmed to the surface, flashing the memories of her coming back to my room and practically giving herself to me. But it was just a dream, wasn't it?

I picked up my cell and texted the one person I could always trust.

Dark shit went down last night. Monte Carlo, Suite 214. Now.

Not even fifteen minutes later, Brax stood in the doorway, hands in pockets, calmer than I could ever hope to be.

A connoisseur of sorts, Brax was an expert in Dark Magic. A fifth-generation warlock. If shit got weird, he's the man to call. Over the decades, he'd helped me out of some crazy situations. As soon as he set foot in the room, I recapped the night before—or the parts I could remember anyway.

I thought about where to begin. *The casino lobby* just after Jacoby's threat.

"I saw her, beautiful, a force. She sat down at the slot machines and I approached her. I asked her what she was. After a few drinks, I brought her back to the suite. I kissed her." I rubbed at the bridge of my nose, trying to clear my head. "Then, Jacoby showed up, looking to fight. She took off, and after they'd gone, I started drinking, hard."

Brax sat on the sofa, eyes pensive, fingers steepled. "Can you tell me more specifics about her?" he asked.

"Dark hair, about this tall." I held two fingers up to where the top of her head met my body. "Beautiful, powerful, but she was hiding something. Darkness, pain . . . madness."

"Are you sure it was the liquor and not magic?"

I stared off toward the bed, wondering why Ivy had used me and for what purpose?

"Dante?" Brax's voice echoed through.

"Sorry." I shook my head and paced the room, "Just confused. I'm never confused. I don't like it."

"How about anything she might have touched? Do you have anything in here which might have her essence on it? A glass she drank from, a piece of her clothing? Anything?"

Brax looked concerned. Now he had me worried.

I looked around the suite and saw the scotch glass with her lip prints on it. "Yes, actually." I collected the glass from the counter and handed it to Brax for inspection.

He turned it in his hands, studying every possible angle. Then, while holding the glass between both hands, one on top, the other on bottom, he closed his eyes and focused. I never interrupted one of his castings. You didn't get between Brax and his work. Not unless you wanted to lose a finger or something even more valuable.

"I see a dark female. Casual clothes? Large, dark eyes?" Brax squinted at me from one eye.

I nodded.

"She's watching you. Last night from the shadows; there's a blank spot, almost shadowing parts of what happened." He focused again "Hours after you passed out, she returned to your room. Convinced the hotel staff to let her in. A glamour, it looks like." He smiled. "Oh, damn, she's good."

Brax always had an appreciation for advanced magic, especially when it came so effortlessly. "After, she came into your room . . ."

He paused for almost a full minute.

"Yes?" I asked impatiently.

"It goes fuzzy, like I'm having telepathic interference or something." Brax looked truly confused.

"Why do you think?"

"Could be an array of reasons." He waved a hand through the air. "She didn't have enough contact with the object, magic being blocked, or the late night I had last night."

He tipped the glass and placed his mouth against it, tasting the spot where Ivy's lips had been. An odd irritation settled into my gut.

"I see a blade . . . and . . . an airplane. Not a reason why. It's too muddled to know what's relevant." He sat back onto the sofa and rubbed his temples. "From all accounts, it looks like she played you. The question now, is why?"

The tattoos along my back twisted and swirled furiously. "Any idea where she's headed?"

Brax tried to reach out one last time, despite the exhaustion threatening to consume him. He started to shake his head and then stopped. "I see a boarding pass." The edges of his eyes tightened. "Looks like Palm Springs."

The desert.

And not just any desert, but the only one near Palm Springs the Dark Fae favored. Right smack on the ley lines.

Shit. I knew exactly where Ivy was.

Shelton Sea had become a major hub over the last twenty years. Hotter than the surface of the sun, the weather sucked ass, but you couldn't' beat the location. So close to the lines, magic could be magnified, manipulated, altered. It drew in all sorts of supernatural beings. Who *wouldn't* want access to them? Ley lines were invisible power markers that conducted magical energy, the equivalent of a magic high.

There were close to 150 ley line locations around the world. It sounded like a lot, but in the scheme of things, it wasn't shit. Ley line territories were fought over harder than any other locations in our world. Whoever headed up the territory had likely sent Ivy, but why?

I slammed my fist against the wall, leaving a visible dent twice the size of a baseball. My temper had clouded all rational thought. I scooped up my bag and threw it down on the massive bed.

Brax hopped up suddenly "Whoa, what are you doing?"

"I'm going to Shelton Sea."

"You don't even know she took anything."

"My point exactly. I don't know. And I need to know."

"Remember where you're going, Dante. The ley lines are complicated places. When's the last time you've been to one?"

Close to a hundred years, but whatever. I was now on a mission—for blood. She had tricked me. Seduced me. Made me believe she wanted me. I had gone along like some horny, desperate teenager. What the hell had gotten into me?

She had. Now I needed to know why.

And then it happened. As if a floodgate was opened. It might have been my anger had turned the key, but a single memory resurfaced. One which sealed her fate. Sealed my own. I saw her, there in the shifting world. It wasn't something I had imagined or even dreamed. She had visited me, drained my powers and done . . . something. Taken something. She would pay—in blood or worse.

"Brax," I said returning to the living room.

"What?"

He was ashen when I turned my fiery gaze on him. My fury had to be something horrifying because I had seen his look on many faces—usually right before I bashed them in.

"She drained me."

Brax rose from the couch. "How? I didn't see it."

"I don't know how. But now it makes sense. The haze, the confusion. She kissed me, that has to be how she did it. How she overpowered me. Some kind of magic in her kiss." I paused. "I... I'm pretty certain I told her I was coming for her."

"That's why you couldn't remember—or at least the physical you couldn't. Your spirit knew, but your body needed time to catch up."

I considered my options for a moment. "I need your help, if you're willing."

"Of course," he said.

"I'm not sure what to expect, but she's powerful, and I imagine her keeper is even stronger."

"Whatever you need." He grabbed his phone out of his back pocket. "Let me make a few calls. Get us as much info as I can."

Twenty minutes later, I'd showered, and Brax returned from pacing outside on the balcony. He plopped onto the couch across from me.

"So?" I asked.

He grabbed an orange from the complimentary basket on the table and peeled the skin. "Your girl is probably property of Bastian Marquis."

The same heat from last night simmered under my flesh at the thought of Ivy belonging to anyone. I shouldn't care. She'd betrayed me, and I wanted revenge now, didn't I? I started to wonder about this Bastian. Maybe he was to blame, and not her, if she was acting under his rule. Regardless, she had broken the cardinal rules—don't drain Dante.

Don't lie to Dante.

Don't cross Dante.

"What is he?"

"Fae."

Seriously, was every one of the assholes I couldn't stand Fae?

"Power?"

"Pretty high." Brax popped a slice into his mouth. "But there isn't much more info out there. Estimates put him at a thousand years old or so. Keeps a relatively low profile overall."

"Do you know where to find him?"

A smug smile lifted his lips. "I do."

"Good." I rose from the couch and made my way toward the bedroom. "We leave immediately."

"We need time, Dante."

I stopped and turned to him. "Time to what?"

"Prepare. Form a plan. Do some research." He ran a hand through his hair. "Acting before thinking is the best way to run into trouble. We can't rush this."

Damn. He was right. "How much time?"

"Couple days, maybe a week."

"A week?" The markings along my arms scorched with impatience. My demon wanted to storm down there, grab Ivy and . . . what? Hell, I didn't know. "Fine, but no longer. I won't risk it."

Brax smiled and grabbed another slice. "Absolutely."

"Good." I headed toward the bedroom to grab my bag and jacket.

"Just so you know," Brax called out, "the place is heavily guarded and locked down with magical protections."

I popped my head out of the room. "Think you can't handle it?"

"No, of course not, but . . ."

"But?"

"Are you sure you want to do this? Go down this road? You could end up right back into the mix, possibly the middle, of the same people you've wanted to avoid."

He was right. In all of my anger, I'd ignored the most pertinent part of this entire situation: exposure. But, if Ivy had been sent by this Bastian, then I was already exposed. I needed to know what she did to me, why, and for who. Nameless enemies were the worst kind to be had.

"Yes, I'm sure."

Brax nodded.

Maybe it was curiosity or because she had even bested him, but whatever the reason, he didn't argue again. The voice in the back of my mind, the one who wanted Ivy no matter the sacrifice, chimed in: *Maybe she had to do it. Maybe she'd been forced. Maybe she didn't have a choice.*

No, she had a choice. But she chose wrong.

CHAPTER 8

Ivy

I stood in the entrance of Bastian's foyer, waiting for him to appear. When I'd come back from Reno last week, Bastian had been away on business. Marla had taken possession of the tiny plastic baggie carrying Dante's vial of blood. She didn't' say much except a polite thank you and Bastian would be in touch soon.

I fingered the small iron blade in my pocket. I hadn't returned it. In fact, I decided to keep it, along with the excess petty cash. I'd spent a decent amount bribing the staff, but if Bastian inquired about his leftover money, I'd needed every bit of it just to get by in Reno. He wouldn't ask. He never did. The 2,000 dollars he'd given me was a barely a drop in his money pool.

Maybe I'd be able to convince one of the local handyman types to take a look at our fridge? Most of the locals were afraid to get too close to us because of Bastian's influence. But I might be able to work some magic.

Ever since Reno, I'd been actively repressing memories of Dante. It happened every time there was a lull at the bar, or a quiet moment at home, or every time I tried to fall asleep. I'd taken to playing solitaire into the night, just to avoid those moments. Because, when I let the silence take over, it always filled with his voice.

Move on, Ivy. If I ever saw him again, I doubt he'd welcome me with open arms.

Bastian appeared at the head of the stairs. Damn, he just had to make an entrance every damn time.

"Ivy," he said, with something passing for sincerity. "It's so good to see you again."

I'd purposely pulled on an old pair of jeans and a comfy sweatshirt for this because I didn't want him getting the wrong idea. Not now. I knew what I'd promised him, but I'd hoped now wasn't the time. I needed fair warning to mentally prepare myself before I got sweaty with Bastian.

For me, tonight served another purpose. I intended to make sure he kept up his end of the bargain and freed my sisters. I knew it would take some kind of magical spell to release them, and I'd hoped it would be quick and painless. He already had what he wanted, now it was my turn.

Besides, I was still off-balance from Reno. From Dante. The thought of sleeping with Bastian, no matter how attractive the man was, didn't sit well with me at present.

"Marla gave you the package I assume?" I said as he approached.

"Yes. You did an excellent job."

I nodded, wrapping my arms about my waist. "It wasn't exactly easy, you know."

"But I'm sure you made it look easy." He smiled and turned toward the hall. "You seem like you could use a strong drink."

Not with you. But I didn't have the willpower to refuse, not right now. I'd tasted Bastian's wine enough times to know it was worth compromising my better judgment. Back at Casa de Crane, we were a Franzia family.

I followed Bastian into the sitting room. At least he wasn't taking me upstairs . . . yet.

As much as I didn't want to face it, I wasn't sure I would be able to say no to him tonight—or any other. I'd made an agreement to allow him to seduce me. Turning my back on my word would have unpleasant consequences.

Even though my encounter with Dante had left me wanting, the thought of a night with Bastian could hardly quench the fires.

"I got what you wanted," I said.

He smiled and poured a Bordeaux into my glass. "Yes, you did."

"So?"

"So?" he repeated.

I hated how he always made me spell everything out. Maybe he hoped I'd forgotten. *As if I could.*

"My sisters? Their freedom? When is that happening?"

"Soon, love. Very soon."

"I don't like ambiguous terms, Bastian. I want a date."

"Very well then, bring them to me tomorrow evening."

The way he looked at me was hungry and questing but nothing like Dante. As he handed me my glass, our fingers touched. They'd touched a thousand times. Could he read the hesitation on my skin?

"Can't you do it without seeing them?"

He shook his head. "Our link is physical, my sweet. I'll need to undue the blood bond with blood."

He'd used terms of endearment with me often, but tonight, he was laying it on thick. Bastian wasn't an unattractive man. By most standards, he'd be considered hot as hell. I mean, if I just met him in a bar—if I didn't know he was the one responsible for making me what I was, for cursing me and my sisters to a half-life in this godforsaken town . . .

But there was no point in imagining the could be's and the might have been's. Bastian's desire washing over me with every stray glance, even in my ratty bumming-around-the-house clothes, had to count for something, right? I didn't owe Dante anything, and It wasn't like this town was crawling with prospects. If I wanted to scratch the unmistakable itch, it might as well be with someone who'd really appreciate it.

"You're beautiful, you know," he said softly.

I laughed. "Yeah. Dressed to impress."

"Stop it." Bastian shook his head, advancing on me, but stopping just short of whatever he wanted to do. Kiss me or shake my shoulders out of frustration, I couldn't be sure.

Instead, he just reached out and touched my cheek. I couldn't help it. I closed my eyes, leaning into his touch like a lonely house cat. I swear I almost purred.

Dante really had left me in a state.

My skin flushed, all the way up the sides of my neck to my ears.

"Bit warm in here for you?" Bastian smiled. "Feel free to shed a layer or two. I won't tell."

Hesitation, only for a moment, held me back. But I reminded myself of two things: One, I'd made an agreement to 'try' with Bastian. And two, I could say no. I could stop at any time. I doubted Bastian would allow me a husband or boyfriend in the future of my forever servitude. Better to gain something, even if it was just hot sex, out of this arrangement.

Thankfully, I was wearing a tee underneath my sweatshirt. I slipped it over my head and set it aside, trying not to think about how out of place my paint-stained relic of a hoodie looked in Bastian's house.

Suddenly he was touching me again but with more purpose this time. His fingers drifted down the side of my face, to my collarbone, pausing there for a moment. His eyes followed.

A loud crash broke the spell between us.

I whirled around, grabbing for the switchblade in my pocket, before I remembered I hadn't brought it with me. For all Bastian's faults, I always assumed I'd be safe when I was with him.

It was then my danger senses tingled with something entirely different. Flames of a memory licked at the corners of my mind.

Dante.

He'd found me.

Bastian stood, strangely calm, as two men stormed into the room. The man with Dante was a stranger to me. Chin-length, deep chestnut hair with touches of blond tied into a knot at his neck. He was the same height as Dante with fairer skin and rich hazel eyes surrounded by thick-rimmed black glasses. They didn't lesson his lethality—they added a hunky villainous flare to his appearance. He surveyed the room with feral precision. Magic surged around him, crackling like a wild bonfire.

I didn't know how he'd found me, or what he intended to do exactly, but this could not end well.

For a moment, Dante just stood there, nostrils flaring, taking in the scene. There I was, standing by my recently discarded sweatshirt. Bastian with his suit jacket off and his tie loosened, two glasses of wine, and . . . yeah, this didn't look good.

"You," he growled finally, his eyes settling on my disheveled appearance. He stalked toward me, sex and fury wrapped together. Damn, he looked incredible in his black shirt and pants. Like some kind of badass dark warrior. The natural reaction would have been to cower down to such a display of alpha male, but never one to conform, I stood my ground.

"Yes?" I answered calmly.

"You . . . succubus." He spat it out like the ugliest word he could imagine. "I should've known." He shook his head before looking at the Fae standing much too close to me. "And I assume this is him?" He gestured in Bastian's general direction. "Your 'protector,'" he mocked.

"Dante, I . . ." I searched for something—anything—to explain, but what the hell was I honestly going to say? Yes, this is him. The man who sent me to manipulate you. Oh, and yes, I did manipulate you, drugged you, stole some of your blood, and then took off without so much as a goodbye.

Nope, I'm officially an asshole. I opted to keep my mouth shut.

"Nothing to say now?" Dante snarled. "What a different tune you were singing only days ago."

Bastian finally spoke. "You know, gentlemen, under normal circumstances, I'd offer you a drink—"

"Nobody asked for your input, Valentino," Dante said.

I would've laughed if the look in his eyes hadn't been so utterly terrifying.

Bastian let out a throaty chuckle. "Strong words for a man who just broke into my home." He tapped a finger to his lips. "I'm quite curious. How did you manage it?"

Dante crossed his arms, the move flexing every defined muscle. He looked to Bastian with total distaste before turning to me. "Did you get what you wanted?"

"What?"

He shook his head. "Still playing coy, Ivy? It doesn't suit you."

"I'm not playing at anything."

Most of my life, I've been required to lie convincingly. Sometimes on the spot, others with more preparation. Right now, Dante's savageness needed to be tamed. He could be bluffing, confused as to what actually happened and looking for me to screw up and give myself away.

"I don't know what the hell you're talking about." I pivoted on my hip. "Look, we had a great time, but my vacation was over, and I had to head home. There's not much else to tell."

"Bullshit."

"Obviously, you think there's something more going on. There isn't."

He pointed at his friend. "Brax over here, saw what you did. I'm here for answers. And I'm here to get back what's mine."

I wanted Bastian to help me out, but he just seemed to be entertained by the whole situation.

"He saw?" I laughed. "Now you're the one talking bullshit. Nobody saw a damn thing because nothing happened."

"Brax is a talented man, Ivy. You're not the only one around here with power."

A pulse of raw energy hit me hard in the gut. Only a taste of what he could truly do. My blood ran cold, but I refused to let my fear or pain show.

"Sounds like your buddy's confused. I don't know." I shrugged through another tremor of his power. "All I know is you came busting in here, probably knocked a few innocent people's heads together to do it—and why? Because you think I stole something from you? What'd I supposedly steal? I'm really curious."

Brax opened his mouth to speak, but Dante glared at him.

"You mean, other than my life force?" He stared me down, willing me to crumble. "I don't know. Only you can answer your question, Succubus."

Again, severe distaste for what I was shot out with the word. I wanted to pretend like I didn't give two shits if he hated the kind of creature in me, but I did. If possible, he'd made me feel even more disgusted with myself than I already was.

"Yeah, that's right." I took a defiant step forward. "I am a succubus, and by definition, it makes me a manipulative, self-serving whore who does what she wants—and who she wants—whenever she wants." I raised my chin. "Sorry your ego got bruised, Dante, but I lost interest. End of story."

"Liar." Dante charged toward me like a raging bull. I didn't know if he intended to kill me or kiss me, but a step from reaching me, he halted. I looked down to see his friend Brax's hand gripping his bicep like a vice.

Bastian finally appeared at my back. "As Ivy has explained, you've made a mistake. The appropriate response would be to acknowledge it and move on."

For the first time since he'd arrived, Dante studied Bastian. "You're the one who sent her. Why don't you acknowledge it and give me back what's mine? Maybe then, I'll let you live. Or at least make your death quick."

Bastian leaned down until his lips grazed my ear. "Stubborn, isn't he?"

"Get the fuck off her."

I didn't know if it was jealousy or anger, but at Dante's reaction, recognition flashed in Bastian's eyes. "Ah, I see." He lowered his head and sniffed the vein along my neck, his attempt to provoke Dante's already overflowing aggression.

Dante looked just about ready to explode, but Brax stepped forward until the four of us formed a tight square. He reached an arm out in front of Dante and spoke to Bastian. "Watch yourself, mate. You don't know us."

"This is my home, *mate.* And as entertaining as all of this has been, I'm going to need you gentlemen to leave. You're clearly unsettling Ms. Crane."

"Ms. Crane?" Dante glanced to me, then laughed at Bastian. "You don't have any idea who you're screwing with, elf. And I'm not going anywhere. Not until I get what I came for." His gaze focused hard and hot on me again.

"I imagined as much." Bastian snapped his fingers and a dozen figures filled the room. I almost leapt out of my own skin. Shit, where did they even come from? By scent, it was evident they were shifters—powerful ones. Just how many creatures did Bastian own?

"Dante . . ." Brax warned as the other man took a step forward, ready to start a massive brawl in the middle of Bastian's expensive antiques.

I knew Dante was powerful, but more powerful than Bastian? I didn't want to risk it. Even though he seemed ready to end me, I couldn't allow him to come to any real harm. Damn mortal emotions.

"Enough already! You both have gigantic dicks, all right? Can everyone calm down now?"

Bastian laughed, Brax smirked, but Dante found no humor in my words. The heavy silence which followed resembled a showdown in the Wild West. I waited for tumbleweeds to blow through Bastian's foyer or a low whistle to chime. He took a measured look at the other men and decided, for the better, to walk away. At least for now.

I couldn't help my internal sigh of relief.

Dante stepped back toward the same hall they'd entered from but abruptly stopped. "Tonight, I let you live. But . . ." He stalked toward, us and Bastian gripped my arm to tug me back. "If I don't have what's mine returned in twenty-four hours, you'll wish you were already dead." He focused the hatred in his eyes on me. "Both of you."

And then, like a freaking rabbit in a hat, they disappeared. One second there—another gone.

I whirled on Bastian. "Well, this is just fucking great!" I shouted. "What the hell am I supposed to do now?"

"No need to do anything," he said, eyes widening slightly at my unbridled rage. "As you can see, they've left. No harm, no foul."

"No harm, no foul?" I repeated in disbelief. "He tracked me down here, Bastian. He knows what I did. What you made me do. Who knows what he's capable of. What about my sisters? He could be headed for them right now!"

"Relax. As you can see . . .," he gestured his hand out wide, ". . . my men are here. They'll monitor my most precious assets. You, Violet, and Jade are chief among them. There's a protocol for this, Ivy. Please. Take a deep breath."

Bastian reached a hand out to calm me, but I slapped it away. "I've been taking deep breaths!" I shouted. "What the hell is wrong with you? Isn't it your job to take care of your property? It never should've gotten this far."

"You're right, actually," Bastian said, his eyes narrowed. "Which raises the question, how did he track you here?"

"Don't turn the tables on me." I hugged myself tightly again but stood my ground. "He told you what he did. His friend has got some kind of crazy psychic powers."

"He's a necromancer, not a psychic."

"A what?"

"More commonly known as a warlock."

"Thanks for the lesson." I paced back and forth. "How did you not see this coming?"

Bastian took in a sharp breath, taking a few steps toward me. I could tell he wanted to comfort me, to touch me, but he didn't quite dare. "Ivy—"

"He threatened me," I said. "You heard him."

"I know," Bastian replied. "I know. And I'm going to ensure he can't make good on those threats. All right?"

I needed to get to my sisters. They'd never used their powers like I had. They weren't ready to deal with the shitstorm headed our way. *Why hadn't I taught them to defend themselves?* Because I'm stubborn and stupid.

"Haven't I always kept you safe?"

"Safe?" I giggled. Yes, I actually giggled like a six-year-old. "You're the one who constantly puts me in danger."

"You're more than capable of taking care of yourself. You've proven that."

"Not against someone like Dante."

"You have to trust me, Ivy."

"No, I did trust you and look where I am now." I grabbed my sweatshirt from the chair and pulled it overhead before storming off.

"Where are you going?" he called out after me.

"Home!"

I wanted to believe everything would be okay. I'd be safe—we'd be safe—but I couldn't. Not after I'd seen the uncertainty in his eyes.

CHAPTER 9

DANTE

I paced our campsite, breathing in the hot desert air, laced with acrid smoke. My nostrils burned with each inhale, but I welcomed the sting.

I'd never wanted to beat the shit out of something as badly as I did right now. Mad was an understatement. I felt *sick*. Repressed rage radiated through every muscle, to the point where I thought I'd explode or retch. The image of Ivy cozied up to the piece-of-shit Fae like a kitten craving milk had done a total mind screw on me.

I'd expected betrayal. Hell—I knew it was coming—and yet, the sight of it surprised me. Smug bastard. He didn't seem shocked to see us burst through the door. Again, images flooded my mind. Ivy's disheveled hair. Her swollen lips. Her breasts pressed against him like . . . like she wanted him. How had I almost slept with her?

Fuck it. It didn't matter. Nothing really mattered.

So then why was I so amped up? *Because she got to you.* One night and this woman had me by the balls. She'd reminded me what it was like to want. To need. To feel alive.

Such a depressing admission was enough to subdue my demon's

fury. I tipped my head left, then right, cracking the overly tight muscles. Sundown had dissolved into nightfall, transforming the dry, orange desert into a glittering dome flecked with stars. I stretched out by the campfire, resting my back against a boulder, and focused energy into my hands.

A miniscule black flame rose out of my palm, the tips flaring with orange as It waved and swirled. I could only manage to double its size before it disappeared again. I needed to get a hold on my emotions if I intended to regain my powers. Brax would be back any minute, and I'd already solved the first part of our problem. We needed leverage over Ivy, and I knew exactly how to get it.

Ivy would live and die for her sisters. They were her weak spot—and my way in. A dickhead move? Certainly, but I'd warned her about revealing herself. And after all, she was the one who'd chosen to become my enemy. The next step was finding the girls. I'd known the moment we had shown up, the three of them would get dropped into hiding by Bastian. The Fae knew what he had, and he had no intention of risking it.

But Brax was a master at finding what others wanted hidden. Between his abilities and my determination, there wasn't a hurdle big enough to stop us.

Motorcycles roared in the distance. A few minutes later, Brax pulled up, followed by Damon, Kylo, and Blaze. I can count the number of people I trust on one hand, and these men were among them. Damon and Kylo were brothers. Rogue dragon shifters who'd never been the kind to take on a clan after their father's sordid past. Blaze was the master vampire over northeast America. The only one of us we considered "legitimate."

I rose from the dirt to greet them. Damon nodded toward me. "What's up, man?" He rushed passed, headed toward the other side of the boulder. No doubt to take a piss.

Blaze smoothed his hair. "Dante." His thick Italian accent had diminished since we'd last seen each other.

Kylo stormed over, a grin spread across his tattooed face before he pulled me into a bear hug. "It's good to see ya, man!"

"All right. All right." I coughed between protests, trying to regain the air Kylo's grip had robbed me of. He may've been half my size, but his dragon blood left him with bone-crushing strength.

Kylo stepped back. "So, Brax here says you got yourself into some deep shit."

Damon appeared at Kylo's side and slapped his brother's back. "And you're surprised? This *is* Dante we're talking about."

"Not my fault." I said

"That's right. . ." Brax said. "This is the fault of a very hot succubus, who got the best of our good friend." He leaned over Damon's shoulder. "How long did it take you to realize she was succubus, Dante?"

"Less time than it would take me to kick your ass."

Brax smiled. "Noted." He turned toward the other men. "Shall we get started?"

We settled in around the fire, and Brax looked to me. "Would you like to do the honors, or—?"

"I'll handle it. How much have you told them?"

"Most of it." He shrugged. "Except for the next step."

I moved closer to the fire, letting the embers and smoke absorb into my demon. "There's only one way to get my property back. We go for Ivy's sisters."

"Ivy?" Kylo asked

"The succubus," Brax answered.

"Ah."

It shouldn't have bothered me, but I hated them calling her that. They meant to demean her by it.

Kylo sat forward. "Why fool around with some chicks? Why not just go for the Fae's house? We could handle him. You'd already done it before—gotten into his house, I mean."

"No." Brax shook his head. "Getting in isn't the problem. It's surviving. He's more powerful than you'd expect and he's got a shifter army at his call."

"If you can't get out, burn the bitch down." Kylo flipped a lighter in his hand. "Who cares, light the whole town up. If there's no place to hide, we won't have to look very hard."

Brax looked to me. His eyes agreed with Kylo.

Sure, it would've been easier to just burn down the whole damn town, but even I had limits. Destroying a bunch of stupid and naïve, but potentially innocent people, to get what I wanted crossed those boundaries.

"No. We're doing it my way."

"You're going through a hell of a lot of trouble to avoid such an option, Dante. Why?" Blaze asked.

The three other men looked to me, the same curious expressions on their faces.

"I'm not here to make a scene. I only want what's mine."

No one spoke. I'd surprised them.

Hell, I'd surprised myself, but truth was truth. But this wasn't just about exposing myself. I didn't want to expose Ivy. Getting into a territory war on top of the ley lines brought attention from all the wrong kind of supernaturals. Betrayal or not, she didn't deserve the hell that would come her way.

Finally, Kylo said, "All right, man. You're the boss." He cracked his knuckles and cupped the back of his head. "You've got a plan then, I assume?"

I smiled. "You bet your ass I do."

Three days had passed and our search continued to come up empty. Ivy and her sisters had gone off the radar. Even their house had been warded. We couldn't get in to gather any of their belongings for Brax, so tracking them required us to use more human methods. The entire town was on some kind of magical lockdown. Blaze, Kylo, and Damon presented their suggestion of burning Shelton Sea to a crisp, but I simply shrugged off the idea.

What was Bastian's endgame? He knew I had no intention of leaving without what I'd came for. How long could this cat-and-mouse chase last? I sent out feelers, using my powers to try and sense the magical source, but nothing happened. Whatever Ivy had done to me, whatever she'd stolen, I wasn't myself. Frustrated and furious, I passed out under the night sky and dreamed of smashing in Bastian's face.

A push-turned-full-on shove woke me the next morning. Brax hovered over me, sweat dripping down his brow, out of breath.

"I found something," he said.

I sat up and rubbed a hand over my face. " What?"

He caught his breath for a moment, then pushed his glasses back up the bridge of his nose.

"Why do you wear those?" I asked before he could answer my previous question.

"What?"

I nudged my chin, "Those."

"My glasses?"

"Yeah, you don't really need them. And you could easily fix your shitty vision with magic, so why wear them?"

"I thought they gave me a refined look. Am I wrong?"

"You look like a pompous asshole."

He chuckled. "If you're done acting like a pompous asshole, I can tell you my news. Unless you'd rather wait?" He started to walk away.

"Get back here." I stood and dusted off my jeans. My muscles ached from too many hours pressed against the hard, uneven ground. Two centuries of living the high life had made me soft.

Brax leaned on the boulder beside me. "Okay, you remember the dude Blaze had mentioned day before yesterday? Leathery face? The human who seemed shifty?"

"Yeah, I thought nothing came of it?"

"Well, turns out, he's not human, and he works for Bastian."

"How's that possible? I didn't sense anything. Neither did you."

"Barrier magic."

I locked my arms across my chest. "Nobody has barrier magic."

"Bastian does, and he's good. No, not just good—really freaking awesome." Brax smiled to himself as if he'd found a new respect for the man. "It's pretty incredible."

"I'm glad you're so impressed."

Brax laughed. "Oh, relax. You're always my number one, *sweetie*."

"Smartass."

"Anyway, turns out Bastian's 'Leather Face' is a ghoul."

This place really was a mecca for the supes.

Brax continued. "He has a small ranch up near the mountains, and his entire property is filled with at least two dozen ghouls hidden behind barrier magic. I'm betting your girls are there."

I hated ghouls. Not only were they strong, but they didn't wound easily. The whole flesh-eating undead trait gave them the ability to take a massive amount of pain and regenerate body parts. One bite and you were screwed. If the infection didn't turn you into one, it would most definitely kill you.

Not even immortals could avoid un-death.

"We need a diversion."

"Exactly." Brax nodded. "And there's another problem. He's got shifters guarding."

"Damn."

"Yeah, but I'm thinking we split up and double the diversion."

"Attack Bastian and the ghouls?"

"Kind of. Make him think we're going straight after what's ours, draw out his resources." He stuffed his hands into his pockets. "Damon and I take the girls, but we do it quietly. I'll use his own magic against him. Set up a temporary illusion where everything's copasetic."

"I need to be there, too."

Brax shook his head. "No way. man, you've got to be at Bastian's. It's the only way he's going to buy into any of it. You go there, act like you're gonna muscle him, and then attempt to bargain."

He was right. Brax could break the barrier magic, and Damon would be able to sift in easily in his vampire shadow form. When you want to end a ghoul, you send in a vampire. And when you want to end a dozen ghouls, you send in a master vampire.

"All right. But I want to move on this quickly."

"When?" Brax asked

"Tonight."

"It's a risk." Brax shrugged. "They're stronger at night."

I shook my head. "Yeah, but a daytime assault, even in a small town like this, leaves too many potential witnesses."

"You're the boss."

Brax called over Kylo, Blaze, and Damon to go over the new plan. We had eight hours to get everything in order and then tonight, we'd go for them.

CHAPTER 10

Ivy

"You know, I thought after a few days, I'd get used to the smell down here, but I can't." Violet tiptoed on a rack, attempting to reach the small cracked window near the ceiling, her voice unnaturally nasally.

I turned the page of the book in my lap. "Don't be such a drama queen."

Violet twisted her head to look at me. "It smells like old fruit and B.O."

"It's not bad," Jade chimed in.

"This place makes our apartment look like the Ritz-Carlton." Violet climbed off the shelf and dropped down onto the couch, crossing her scuffed Doc Martens at the heel. "How long exactly are we supposed to stay down here?"

After Dante's threat, we'd been shuffled that very night to a property on the eastern edge of Shelton. A small home hidden up in Rayne Mountain. We weren't chained or locked in a cell, but we definitely didn't feel like guests.

"I don't know." I said.

"I'm not asking you, I'm asking Wrinkles."

"Shhh!" Jade's wide eyes looked over her shoulder to our ghoul babysitter.

I'd seen him only a few times around town. He mostly kept to himself and I'd never heard him speak. I honestly didn't know if he even could.

Violet grabbed an old baseball off the floor and tossed it over her head. "How is it you get trips and money, and we get a cramped ten-by-ten cellar?"

"Trips and money? Seriously Vi? I went one time to Reno and the rest of it's been within fifty miles of Shelton." I snapped the book shut. "And as far as the money, you know exactly where it goes. Bills, groceries, savings . . . everything."

I couldn't blame Vi for being angry. We weren't asked to come here we were told. I may have been used to following Bastian's orders, but they weren't.

"So what happens if this dude you pissed off doesn't leave? What if he's here for the next three months? We're just gonna live in a dirty cellar?"

I sighed. "Look, I'll do everything I can to get us out of here as soon as possible, but I'm not a miracle worker."

Violet balled up a piece of old newspaper and threw it over the ghoul's shoulder. "Wrinkles."

"Stop calling him that," Jade tried to whisper under her breath.

"He doesn't even speak or understand."

Jade came over and sat beside me, her eyes glancing to our stoic babysitter. "How do we know him and his 'friends' aren't going to eat us?"

"Because I'd never let that happen."

"Oh, yeah?" Violet yelled from across the room. "Are we going to get a bit more clarity on how you can protect us?"

I stood and circled the room. "Maybe."

"Good." She swung her feet over the sofa and slammed them onto the dusty concrete floor. "Because I'm sick and tired of the secrets."

"So am I."

"Okay, so tell us, tell me. What's really going on? Who are we hiding from? And what does Bastian want with you, with us?"

"I—"

"I want to protect you, Ms. Crane. All of you." Bastian stood in the doorway, dressed in a black suit and gray tie. Where in the hell had he been? Or where was he going? There wasn't a single place in Shelton, or near it, requiring anything even close to his formal attire. And I really doubted he'd gotten dressed up to visit us.

"Holy shit."

It took me a minute to realize who had spoken. We'd never heard such words out of Jade's mouth. If I hadn't been there to see it myself, I wouldn't have believed it.

The first time I saw Bastian, I'd had the same reaction. No doubt my sisters were taken aback when their mysterious monster turned out to be an exceptionally handsome man. Well, Fae, but you know what I mean.

"Ladies." Bastian stepped farther into the room, his golden hair smoothed back in his usual style. He grabbed a folding chair, wiped the base with a towel, and sat. "I understand you're upset. Confused. Perhaps even angry. Let me offer you my sincerest apologies. If there were any other way to keep you from harm, I would have chosen it."

Violet raised her chin and leaned back against the wall. The "Fuck you" radiating in her stare was enough to unnerve even the most confident of men. But Bastian was so much more than a man, and neither of my sisters had the slightest clue of who they were dealing with. The look in Jade's eyes had me worried. She didn't appear fearful. If anything, she seemed curious about him—intrigued even.

Hell *no*. I had to put an end to this. Immediately.

I stepped intentionally between him and my sisters. "Why are you here?"

"I wanted to check on your well-being."

Bullshit. He didn't come all the way over here, dressed fancy, just to check on us. I crossed my arms and waited.

"And . . . I need to speak with you, privately."

"What about?"

"I'd rather not involve your sisters."

I glanced over my shoulder. Violet now sat beside Jade on the couch, both of them focused on Bastian and me.

"Outside?" I asked.

Bastian nodded and extended his arm out wide for me to lead the way. I turned back to my sisters. "I'll be right back. Don't move."

Hot desert air smacked into my face as we exited the cellar. Most times, I detested the constant warmth against my skin, but tonight, I savored it. Stars speckled across the midnight-blue sky, creating a perfect silhouette of the surrounding mountains.

As much as I wanted to bask in the hot, musty-free air, I wasn't there to enjoy the scenery. I took three more steps from the door and turned to face Bastian. "What's going on?"

He tucked his hands into his pockets. "I need you to go to Porter's this evening."

"Why?"

"I've received word of a business contact arriving. I need you there to gather some information."

"Wait. I'm sorry." I put my hand into the air between us. "You want me to leave the safety of this place—and my sisters—so I can be your lap dog for the night and potentially cross paths with the man who, in case you forgot, threatened to kill me? No way."

"You'll be protected there. Porter warded the bar. Not even my men can enter."

"No."

"This isn't a request, Ivy. Need I remind you, you are still indebted to me."

I stepped into his space, my finger pointed at his chest. "Last time I checked, you were supposed to remove my sisters from the bond. Which has yet to happen. As far as I see it, you're the one who owes me."

Due to Dante's interruption, Bastian hadn't undone the magic binding my sisters to him. Now I wasn't certain if he ever would. He'd probably back out of the entire agreement, citing that the risks were too great now.

Bastian sighed. "Ivy, this man isn't just a threat to me, but to you and your family as well. I need to know his purpose. Only you can obtain that for me."

The concern edging his eyes made him appear tired and weary. The Fae never looked anything but exceptional. This was bad.

"Why is he here?" I asked.

"I don't know." He smoothed his hair again. "But it's important that we find out."

Once again, I found myself with no other choice but to do as Bastian asked. I exhaled. "Fine, but you and your ghouls better keep my sisters safe. If anything happens to them, I swear to god, I'll kill you all."

"I 'd expect nothing less."

Threatening a Fae was always a risky move, but I didn't care. Not tonight. "Good, because I mean it, Bastian."

"I said I understood."

"Between a rock and hard place" had become the only way to describe my life anymore. I didn't want to add another enemy to my ever-growing list, but if this man truly was a threat, I needed to listen to Bastian.

I paced a few steps, then turned to him. "All right, what do you want me to do?"

CHAPTER 11

DANTE

At ten o'clock p.m. exactly, Brax set out to grab the girls, while I headed for Bastian's, Kylo and Blaze in tow.

To my disappointment, he wasn't there. Instead, his assistant, Marla, offered to reach out to her boss and get this entire situation squared away before things got out of hand. I played my part, brooding and barely able to keep my anger at bay, but I knew Bastian wouldn't be returning whatever he took.

The not knowing still annoyed me.

I knew everything.

I checked my watch again. Brax and Damon were twenty minutes late for our rendezvous. What the hell was taking so long? There's no way that leather face and his ghouls had overpowered the two of them.

Kylo sat on a rock at the cave's edge of our campsite, toying with the phone in his hand. "At what point do we go for them? Another ten minutes?"

I cracked my neck. "They'll be here."

"You think they were able to get shit done with no problem?" Blaze asked.

"I do. There'd be more activity if they hadn't."

In the distance, motors rumbled. The ball of tension in the pit of my stomach eased.

Brax and Damon rolled to a stop just outside the entrance, blindfolded figures strapped to each of their bikes.

"Any problems?" I asked before noticing they were down one female. The most important one. "Where's Ivy?"

"She wasn't there."

I let the words soak in. "Well then, where the hell is she? What did her sisters tell you?"

Brax shifted one of the girls off his seat. "They won't say."

"So, make them." My tattoos ignited, as irritation slithered up my spine.

"Dante," He guided me a few steps away and spoke low, glancing back toward the girls. "Look. Her essence was all over that room. If she was there, it was recently. I'd say within hours."

It took everything in me to remain calm. My demon wanted nothing more than to knock Brax off his feet with a punch directly to the jugular. Fortunately for him, I was practiced at self-control.

I inhaled slowly, then released it. "The plan doesn't work without Ivy, Brax."

"So we adjust."

"And the Illusion? It's intact?"

"As long as he doesn't try to interact with anybody, we're good."

"Then what's your big idea?" I asked.

"We find Ivy. I've got a dozen recent objects she's touched filtered into my senses. We wait for things to calm down, then we go for her, make her play ball."

"What about them? Are they gonna play ball?" I nudged my head toward Ivy's sisters being guided into the cave by Damon and Blaze.

"Somewhat combative. One of them is a total pain in the ass, but after we gagged her, it wasn't a problem."

Once far enough inside, Damon lowered the girls until they clumsily landed on the dirt floor. Dust scattered up into the air and flecks illuminated over the fire blazing in the center of the cavern. Their hands were bound and mouths gagged in addition to the blindfolds. It was important to create as much confusion as possible. I'd noted twelve caves like this just in the surrounding twenty miles. They'd have to be very, very good to figure out where we were.

"Take the bonds off their mouths and remove the blindfolds." I moved until I stood just over them, arms crossed over my chest.

As soon as Brax touched her, muffled yelling started from the one with darker hair. She tried to push away from him, kicking and clawing at him, but her hands were still tied.

The second the gag dropped, she started in. "Get off of me." She nearly bit Brax's fingers off.

"Relax," he said, snatching his hand back before she could sink her teeth into it.

"Relax? Seriously? You just tied us up and kidnapped us. Relaxing is the last goddamn thing I'm going to do."

Like Ivy, she had jet-black hair and tan skin. A wild fire danced in her violet eyes. And just like Ivy, she looked like trouble. The other was more demure, with dull brown hair, but beautiful green eyes to compensate. She either looked like her father or wasn't completely Ivy's sister; the other one, too, for that matter.

"No one's going to hurt you," Brax reassured.

"Excuse me if I'm not convinced of that." Hands still bound, she reached over to her sister and gently squeezed her hand, almost moving herself into a protective position. "Do you know who we are? Who you're messing with?"

While Brax was being the good cop, I decided to flaunt a little bad cop. "Which one of you is Jade and which is Violet?"

The one with dark hair set her jaw and lifted her head to me, locking eyes and holding them. It was quite impressive, given her current predicament. She was in no way in a place of power, but she was holding herself as if she were.

"I'm Violet," she growled through clenched teeth. "Who the hell are you?"

"I'm the one asking the questions, sweetheart." I lowered my head until I was barely an inch from her face. "And you're the one who's answering them. Got it?"

She blew a strand of black hair that fell in her eyes. Brax leaned against the wall to her side, arms tucked into his pockets as he watched her with too much focus. Shit. I turned and looked at Kylo, Damon, and Blaze. They were scattered about the cave, but close enough to overhear, each of them watching the two beautiful creatures intently. What was it with these sisters? One glance and they'd captivate any man in the room.

"Are you him?" the quiet one asked from over Violet's shoulder.

"Him?"

"The guy. The one Bastian was protecting us from," Jade stated.

Violet laughed. "Protecting us? Nobody protects us Jade, except us. You know that."

"Are you here to kill us?" Jade whispered.

I looked at Brax, who tore his eyes away from Violet long enough to face me. We'd never been the heroes. I'd never hurt someone who didn't have it coming. Right now, this wasn't about truth, this was about perception. I had to know what Ivy had stolen from me: why she'd done it and how to get it back.

I shook my head. "If I wanted you dead, I wouldn't have had you brought here." I paced across the cave, keeping my eyes on them. "Your sister stole something from me. You're going to help me get it back."

"I'm not doing a damn thing," Violet snapped.

"We couldn't even help you if we wanted to," Jade argued. "We don't know anything."

"Do you know who I am?"

Violet raised her chin. "We know enough."

"Good. Then you know I'm not screwing around." I flicked my hand open. A flare of flame and smoke sprouted from my palm. "Fortunately for you both, I don't need you to do anything, except listen and do as your told." I turned and faced the fire, giving them my back. "If you can manage to do that for the next couple of days, you'll both live—and so will Ivy."

"And if we don't listen?"

I had to give Violet credit. She had as much moxie, if not more, then most men I knew.

"Then I have no use for you," I stated flatly.

Silence filled the cave as they weighed their options. Not that there were many options.

I heard a scuffling as one of them rose. I didn't have to figure out who. "All right. But you better not lay a hand on either of us—or our sister."

"Agreed." I turned to Brax. "You'll take Jade. Damon will take Violet. Blaze can trail you both, and Kylo's with me." The second eldest Crane sister had made too strong of an impression on Brax, and I needed to keep them separated.

Damon clutched Violet's arms, and she stiffened, refusing to move. "Wait, where are you taking us?"

"Out of town. It's the safest place for you. Once I get what's mine, you'll see your sister again. Perhaps even sooner."

She and Jade exchanged a tight glance. "We can't go."

"I'm not asking."

"I'm not talking about our will here," she argued.

"Enough!" I roared over her voice. For fuck's sake, this chick could argue with the best of them. "Brax, bind her mouth again until she learns the value of silence."

Brax looked back at the pair and then to me. Whatever he wanted to say, he kept to himself. A few minutes later, Violet's protests were muffled again and when Jade tried to argue, I'd told him to do the same to her. Their gags remained tight enough to do the job but not so much as to do any real damage. I wouldn't admit it aloud, but I knew it would upset Ivy, and for that reason alone, I couldn't do them harm.

As we drove to the edges of town, Jade rode on the back of Brax's bike, her arms tied about his waist with rope. Violet rode behind

Damon. She gripped the seat, refusing to hold onto Damon's waist with the cord he'd given her bound hands. When we approached the city limits, magical energy pulsed and a crackle of light and power erupted. Seconds later, the girls flew backward, like plastic bags through the air. They hit the asphalt hard, smothered grunts forced from their lips at the impact.

"Holy shit." I turned the bike too suddenly, not accustomed to the sudden magical flux, and dropped it. Forgetting the metal beast for the moment, I rushed to make certain they were all right. I was trying to scare the shit out of them, not actually get them killed.

Kylo and Blaze rolled up beside me. "What just happened?"

"I don't know." I said, before I stormed across the road.

Anyone human would've broken their neck or worse, but both girls, aside from a few bruises and scratches, appeared fine.

Now that was really interesting. Were they like Ivy? Or something else?

Brax knelt down and undid the binds and gags still wrapped around them. I hadn't exactly approved the decision, but after what they'd just been through, I figured a few allowances were in order.

"What was that?" I asked.

Violet turned her steely gaze on me. "I told you, you idiot. We can't leave." Her rage was a force to reckon with. She turned and reached out to her sister. "Jade, you okay?"

Jade wiped at the pebbles impaled into her palms, blood and dirt smearing the front of her jeans with each swipe. "Yeah, I'm okay."

I kneeled down in front of Violet. "Are you going to explain?"

She licked at the bloodied cut on her lip and turned.

"I said, explain. Now."

"Dante, give her a minute, man," Brax fired at me.

I cocked an eyebrow at him, and he looked away, not willing to stare me down.

"We can't leave. Not me. Not Jade. Not Ivy. I don't know why, and I can't tell you any more than that. Bastian controls it. Controls us."

Brax glanced from Violet to me, recognition lighting in his eyes.

"He's got a blood-tie to them. They're charmed somehow, making it so they can't flee."

It all made sense. Especially after Ivy's comments in Reno. *There is no escape,* she had said. Maybe in more ways than one for her.

Brax pulled me off to the side as the others helped the girls up. "What's the plan now? Go back to the cave?"

I looked at the stars. They were less visible tonight than last. "No, we need to keep moving. Choose another spot, somewhere with daytime coverage." I glanced to Brax again. "You'll need to mask our presence as well. We can't risk being found before the plan plays out. Bastian can't know the girls are gone."

"He won't. I'll take care of it."

"Good. I—"

I cocked my head to the side, unable to speak as awareness hit me in the gut. A presence returned, simmered inside of me. A presence mingled with my own energy—Ivy.

I jogged back across the road, grabbed my bike and raised it upright.

"Where are you going?" Brax asked, following me.

"To deliver to the news."

"What news? And to who?"

"Ivy." I slipped onto the black leather seat. "She just resurfaced, and I know exactly where."

CHAPTER 12

Ivy

Everything was normal. Everything was fine. Nothing was wrong.

If I said it enough times, maybe it would be true.

Bastian dropped me off at Porter's thirty minutes ago. Before he left, he tried, *and* failed, to reassure me that my sisters and I were safe. When I asked where he was going, he stated he'd be out of town for a couple of days and would return on Saturday. At that time, he expected a full report on this uninvited imp entering his territory. I had to admit, Bastian's optimism that I'd still be alive by then left me somewhat hopeful.

Porter didn't make a big scene when I walked through the door. Instead, he nudged his head and went straight back to work. I took my place behind the bar, cleaning off the counter and replenishing drinks as if the last two weeks hadn't happened.

A light crowd tonight meant I'd easily spot this newcomer. Not that it would've been too difficult with more people. An imp's energy was much like a succubus'. It would be impossible to not sense him. Besides, Bastian said the man had strawberry blonde hair and yellow eyes resembling a horned owl. I doubt I'd miss someone who looked like *him*.

Besides Marla and Lila, Porter never allowed Bastian's people inside. He always spoke of his bar as neutral territory. Showing favoritism in any one direction in the supernatural world brought on too many headaches. Now I understood why.

To avoid the rising tension, Porter had warded his bar from the conflict. No one involved in any of the current drama was getting inside. I took comfort in that. Even so, I still wanted all of this to end. To go back to my tedious normalcy.

I wonder what Dante would do if I just stole the vial back and gave it to him? Would he even believe it was all I had taken? Would he forgive me and leave us alone? Did I want him to? The logical parts of my brain told me it didn't matter, while the tug in my chest reminded me we still had a strange connection, no matter how much I wanted to pretend we didn't.

Just as I rinsed out some glasses, the tug grew stronger. Almost physically jerking me toward the door.

It wasn't possible.

I knew Dante was coming right before he walked in the door. Not enough time to prepare or do anything but stare at him as he approached.

How had he managed to break Porter's ward? From what I understood, Porter had been taught the incantation by a direct descendant of the Salem witches.

Too involved in their own shit, not a single person glanced at the sexy demon who'd just walked in. His black-on-black outfit and dark, seductive eyes made my stupid stomach flutter like some pubescent teenager. Apparently, you still wanted to screw someone, even after he threatened your life.

He sat down in the empty corner. Without glancing in my direction, he set a wrinkled bill on the bar.

Fuck. Fuck. Fuck.

Relax! Breathe Ivy!

My ego—and his predator instincts—couldn't see me falter. I steadied myself, crossed the bar, and leaned against the back counter. "If you're here to kill me, I'm not gonna make you a drink, so put your money away."

He looked up from under his thick black lashes, "I'm here to talk."

"Talk? I thought you were done talking." False bravado, people. It's the only way to survive.

"Do you have zero sense of self-preservation?"

I shrugged. "Probably. But then again, I'm not the one who walked into a bar where I wasn't welcome. How did you get through the wards?"

"Bastian has his tricks—I have mine."

"He's going to find out, you know?"

"I'm not worried."

"You should be."

Dante sat forward. "He should be."

I practically suffocated on the surge of magic enveloping the air around us. Raw power crackled and popped like embers on a wild blaze, feverish and hot to the touch. When he dropped the power display, I looked around, expecting everyone in the room to be just as thrown off as I was, but they weren't. In fact, no one seemed to have noticed Dante's presence at all.

Finally, it dawned on me. "No one else can see you, can they?"

He didn't answer me, he simply smiled and leaned back into his chair. "Are you going to get me a drink?"

I wiped at my sweat-covered face, "Seriously?"

"I said I wasn't here to kill you."

He had a point. I picked up an empty tumbler, swallowing down all the things I wanted to scream at him. "So, why are you here then?"

"You know why."

"I didn't steal anything," I murmured, glancing over my shoulder as I filled his glass with bottom-shelf whiskey and a huge handful of ice. "I told you."

"Stop," he said flatly. "No more lies."

I handed him the tumbler, and he frowned at my obvious attempt to destroy his drink. "Have you given any thought to how you're going to steal it back? Because, if you haven't, now might be a good time."

"Oh?" My throat itched, drier than the desert wind. "And why is that?"

Dante reached into his pocket, and I instinctively took a step back. But he just produced a little black rectangle. A phone.

Then he held up the screen for me to see. I scrunched my nose and leaned closer. Violet and Jade, bound and gagged.

"How? Why?" I shook my head, trying to keep my shit together. "What did you do to them? Where are they?"

"Safe, and they'll remain that way, as long as we come to an understanding."

I would've slammed a fist into his jaw if I didn't care about drawing attention to myself. "You're a real asshole, you know that? Gagging two innocent women."

"The only reason they're gagged is because they can't hold their tongues. Kind of like their big sister."

"They have nothing to do with this."

"As I've told you, they're not in danger. Not yet at least. As long as you listen, my men will keep them safe. Safer than your Bastian ever could."

"He's not . . ." Mine, I almost said, but what a ridiculous thing to fixate on right now.

Dante tucked the phone back into his pocket. The image of my kidnapped sisters would be burned into my mind's eye until the end of time, so it didn't really matter. Although I did want to smash the thing, out of principle.

My whole mind and body raged with indignation, anger, shame, fear, and the lust for revenge.

But through it all, the pull never stopped.

The connection. Dammit. How could it still be so strong?

"What understanding do we need to come to?" I knew that to go against Bastian was a risk, but right now, Dante had my sisters, so he made the rules.

He took a sip. "You know what I want. I need your help getting it."

"You realize that you're asking me to trade one bad situation for another, right? If you don't end me, Bastian will."

"Bastian doesn't need to know."

"How? Wo— "

"Ivy?" Porter stood to my left, brows furrowed as he looked from me to the corner barstool. Clearly, he couldn't see Dante either. "Everything okay?"

"Yeah, of course." I grabbed the towel and wiped at an imaginary spot.

"What are you doing?"

"I'm just thinking aloud." I laughed. "Sorry if that was weird."

He didn't seem convinced of my sanity, but he nodded his head, grabbed a case off the floor, and headed for the storeroom.

Anger boiled within me, reaching a tipping point that had me flinging the towel against the bar the moment Porter was out of sight. It only upset me more that the lightweight fabric hadn't hit with a resounding thud.

"How about you go fuck yourself." It wasn't a request, though I knew from the smug curl of Dante's lips he wasn't about to give me what I'd wanted.

I stepped into the back office, my well-intentioned move to separate myself from him ceasing the moment I heard the click of his steps on my heels.

"Did I not say it loud enough?" I spun, my jaw nearly cracking with how rough my teeth grounded together.

He drew closer, heat rolling off him in droves.

"I believe," he mocked, "you said to go fuck myself. But it would be far more fun to—"

I aimed square for his jaw and swung. My fist carried with it all the tension and unbidden attraction welled up inside of me. One hit would free me, make me forget everything this man did to me.

Dante was too quick and too skilled. My fist caught in the curl of his fingers, his jaw left irritably untouched as he used my own throw for leverage and nearly yanked me off my feet. He spun me, and my back collided against his chest. The heat of his breath brushed my neck like a small blanket of hot, delicious smoke.

Fire and bourbon.

I needed an escape. I flung my elbow back, slamming hard into his gut. A rush of air whooshed from him, fluttering my hair. I twisted under his grip, but as I turned around my back hit the wall, and I had nowhere to go.

He rushed at me, his forearm slamming against my upper chest. I was pinned entirely between the wall and the weight of him. Anger burned from my eyes, but I knew when I looked up into the smoky mirror of his own, we had both lost.

His lips crashed over mine with vengeance, staking their claim with every sweeping press of his tongue that begged for entrance. I hated him, and I wanted him, and the volatile mix had me burying my fingers roughly into the thick of his hair as my lips parted in response.

His rough hands swept down my body, their heated touch drinking in my every curve until they halted on the pull of my hips. It was there, he tugged me closer, sending an exhale of utter lust slipping from my lips into the open of his mouth.

Not a single protest left me as his fingers dug into my hips and lifted me from the ground. I couldn't protest, not when he was the oxygen and I the flame.

My legs flung around him, clinging with an all-consuming need to be closer. His lips pulled away, their trailing graze paused on the hollow of my neck. A hiss of a breath slipped from between my teeth as I clung to him harder and tasted the remnants of him in a quick sweep of my lips.

He slammed me down on Porter's desk.

Notebooks and pens jammed uncomfortably into my back, but none of that mattered as Dante's hands ran back up my form. They dragged over the curve of my chest taking with them the responsive arch of my back that only begged him closer into the catch of my legs.

His hands may have been on me, all over me, but I needed more.

My fingers curled into the collar of his shirt and yanked him back against me in a crushing kiss that belied any semblance of control I'd had. He settled atop me, his weight alone enough to shallow my breath. The heady, husky scent of him enveloped me. I couldn't breathe it in enough times.

I caught his lower lip between my teeth in a firm tug. His hips shifted, leaving me desiring far more than an anchor to hold.

This entire situation was insane, but I needed him inside of me.

When I adjusted to get a better angle, something jabbed uncomfortably into my inner thigh. I tried to ignore it under the fervor of Dante's lips, but it continued to press awkwardly.

Suddenly, I realized what it was. Dante's damn phone filled with images of my sisters bound and gagged.

Yup. I'm a total and utter head case. Ready to screw the man who had threatened my life and currently had my sister.

My senses returned, and I shoved at him. "Get off of me," I snapped, breathless.

Dante froze, caught the seriousness in my gaze, and extracted himself from me.

I loathed just how much I desired to pull him back. I couldn't make eye contact with him as I pointed toward the door.

"Just go." I sat upright, my eyes focused on his boots.

"Ivy . . . I'm—"

"No. We're not talking about it. Just go."

He retreated to the door, then stopped. He rubbed a hand over his neck and cursed before he turned back to me. "Look, what I said earlier still stands. Bastian doesn't need to know you're doing this for me."

"I'm not doing anything for you. Anything I do is for my sisters."

His jaw ticked. "You know what I meant."

"How could you possibly think that Bastian won't find out? He knows everything. I'm sure he knows that my sisters are gone already."

Dante stepped forward. "No. He doesn't."

"How?"

"It's taken care of. As far as Bastian knows, the girls are still tucked safely inside the ghoul's basement. Right now, that's all you need to know. But if you want to end all of this, you'll find me—and you'll do it before Bastian returns."

He moved closer until he stood in front of me, his legs brushing mine against the desk. "Thanks for the drink, sweetheart." He took a twenty out of his wallet and dropped it onto my lap. "Think about what I said."

Gods, he still smelled incredible. Needing to keep my shit together, I reached for my last line of defense—sarcasm. "Can I have your business card?" Knowing him, the title on it would read: Badass Warrior.

He smiled and a dimple formed in his cheek.

Stupid handsome face.

"I have a feeling you'll find me when you're ready."

I don't know how long I sat there, staring at the door after he'd left. I was an emotional clusterfuck. Needy, unsatisfied, angry, embarrassed, and totally confused. What the hell had just happened? Did I really almost have sex with my sisters' kidnapper? Gods, I was a thousand times more jacked up than I'd ever thought possible.

I didn't have much time to ponder my questionable sanity before Lila stormed in, like a tempest in a teacup.

"I need to talk to you. Now!"

I don't know whether it was Dante's latest reveal, our almost sex, or if I'd reached my max of emotionally taxing crap, but I didn't bother protesting. Instead I followed her outside.

"Where the hell are they?" she almost shrieked, as soon as we hit the parking lot.

"Keep it down. We don't need the whole damn town knowing our business."

"I don't care who hears." She grabbed at my bicep, her fingernails digging into my skin. "Do you understand what you've done, Ivy? Do you understand what could happen to them? They could die because of you!"

Tears stung at the corners of my eyes, and I willed them not to fall. Only Lila could make me feel like this, and I hated myself for it. Freaking mothers. They could cure you—or kill you—with a single sentence.

"What do you care now?" I snapped back. "You've never taken care of them, of us. In my opinion, it's none of your business."

"Bastian won't tell me what happened." She twisted her hands anxiously. "Nobody will tell me what happened. Just that the girls are under protection, and I can't see them."

To be honest, I'd never seen her like this. Since when did she start worrying about us, or them, or anyone else, for that matter?

Don't let her manipulate you, Ivy. This is what she does.

"You're pretty good at playing the worried mother, but where were you when they needed dinner? When they woke up from a nightmare at two am?" It took all my fortitude to hold back the years of rage. "I was the one who took care of them, Lila. Just me. Nobody else. Certainly not you. So, stop pretending like you care now."

Lila's whole body quivered. "If I'd known you were going to use it to play the martyr," she snarled, "I never would've let you care for your sisters, who you supposedly love so much. I had no idea it was such a burden for you."

"I was a kid, too! Or, at least, I would've been if you ever gave me the chance!"

Lila took in a sharp breath. "I never claimed to be the perfect mother," she said finally. "But I don't want to see my daughters get hurt. Is that so impossible for you to wrap your selfish head around?"

"I'm doing everything I can."

"Well, then let me help."

Okay, now this had to be a joke.

"Who are these men? What do they want? I know Bastian sent you on some secret errand. Can you get them what they want and undo this whole mess?"

"I'm trying," I repeated. "But it's complicated. He wants something that I can't give him. Something I took from him."

Don't ask me why I chose to explain myself. Like I've said, I'm all jacked up.

"So, give it back," Lila said, like it was the easiest thing in the world. "Steal it. You can do that. Use your powers. Get Bastian in such a state that he doesn't know his own name anymore. I know you can do it."

"You're awfully eager to pimp me out," I snapped. "I'm not entirely convinced it would work."

"Understand this. If anything happens to your sisters, I will never, ever, forgive you."

Funny. That was basically the same threat I'd given Bastian, except I'd also promised to kill him.

I couldn't hold it back anymore. "It's not my fault!" I shrieked, pushing her back from me. To my surprise, she didn't react or even try to hold her ground. She stumbled back instead, letting most of her weight fall against the exposed brick of the bar's outside walls.

I realized she was crying and stood there, breathing hard. I didn't know what else to do.

Finally, she spoke. "I know I failed more often than not. But I did try, Ivy. You have to understand. I wanted to give you all a better life. Bastian offered that."

"A better life?" I echoed, in disbelief. "You *gave* us to a stranger. You let him basically kill us and bring us back as freaks." I shook now. "Don't you dare lie about your reasons. You did what you did for you and no one else."

She looked up at me, mascara streaking down her face. "Yes, I did it for me . . . and for you. Maybe you'll never believe me, but it's the truth. This world is horrid and painful and shitty." She took a deep breath in. "Bastian offered the chance to be better, do better, have better."

Holy hell. She really did believe her own bullshit.

"You honestly thought we'd be better off as pawns in some mad Fae scientist's experiments?"

"What would you rather have? Living in a one-bedroom trailer with an alcoholic and no future? Those were our only options, Ivy. I gave you and your sisters something most people would kill for. Magic. Actual magic. You can wrap the whole world around your little finger, and you've only ever seen it as a curse. All you can do is complain. You were never going to have the normal life you wanted. A golden retriever. A house with a white picket fence. PTA meetings. This was our way out, Ivy."

I took a deep breath. My whole life, I'd been trying to understand how and why my mother put us through all this bullshit, and I was finally starting to get it. She idolized the Fae. To her, magic of any kind —even as indentured servants—was better than a mundane life without it.

Not the apology I'd hoped for, but at least she somewhat acknowledged her fuck up.

"Look, I'm going to figure this out. I'm going to get them back. Safe. No matter what. Just give me time."

I went back inside without another glance in her direction.

I waited through the end of my shift for Bastian's imp to show up. Two more hours had passed and the imp he claimed was 'in his territory' hadn't appeared. I didn't know whether he'd gotten wind that Bastiaan was looking for him, or if he'd been smart enough to hide himself, but whatever the reason, I was grateful that I had nothing to report back to Basitan.

Instead, I gathered my keys and headed straight for Dante to put an end to all of this.

CHAPTER 13

DANTE

Two hours after my visit to Porter's, Ivy's magic reached out and summoned my soul. I hated to admit how good the sensation was, like a long, sensual caress against my skin. The fact that I'd almost screwed her on her boss' desk didn't minimize the effect she had on me. It only magnified my aching desire for this woman.

I shook it off and made my way away from the cave. Ivy's sisters sat deep inside, guarded by Blaze, Damon, and Brax. Kylo stood sentinel outside.

"Need backup?" he asked following me a few steps down the rocky hillside.

I shook my head. "No." This time, I held the advantage.

Twenty-minutes later, she stood at the edge of our campsite, arms wrapped about her waist, as her raven hair blew with the tepid evening breeze. I'd noticed the action before. It was her *tell*. Even with a cocky brow raised, uncertainty plagued her.

"You're a dick."

Not what I expected her to say, but an interesting start. "Only when I'm required to be."

"You wanted to talk." She kicked the dirt. "So, talk."

She waited several minutes, expecting me to answer, but I remained silent. I wanted to make her uneasy. I took the moment to study her in again. Her face remained flushed and damp from the heat, reminding me of the way she looked lying across Porter's desk. I was a lost man.

She exhaled, impatience growing as the minutes ticked on. "I want to see my sisters."

She'd barely looked me in the eyes. Christ, was she blushing? I didn't move from the rock resting against my back. "First, we talk, then if I like what you have to say, you can see them."

"No. Because my offer's null if they aren't okay." She said.

Fuck, everything was a chance to barter for her. And I loved—and hated it—when she argued with me.

"No."

Her beautiful dark eyes flashed wide. "No?"

"I'm not negotiating on your terms anymore, sweetheart. You're going to have to bite your tongue, put your ego aside, . . ." I waved a hand through the air, ". . . whatever you want to call it."

"You're loving this, aren't you?" She said, "Holding shit over my head."

"All of this could've been avoided if you'd just admitted what you stole from me and why, but instead—"

"Blood."

"What?" I asked, my smart-ass reply dissolved at her admission.

"I took a vial of your blood."

"Why?" How the hell did she manage that? No one could get to my blood, so how did she pull it off?

"Because Bastian told me to."

A pang of jealousy stabbed me in the stomach, burning through me. "And you always do what he tells you to, reasons be damned? Consequences be damned?"

She shook her head and looked off toward the distant mountains. "You don't get it. Maybe your life works like that, but mine doesn't."

"You're right. I think for myself. Act for myself."

Angry eyes snapped back to mine. "I want to see my sister's. Now."

"We're not done talking."

"We can keep talking after I see them."

I mulled over her request. Certainly, the less "Fuck you, Ivy" part of me, wanted to see her smile, see her happy. But the angry demon stirring in my chest wanted to torture her a little longer, a little further.

The less "Fuck you" part won.

"You get one minute. Follow me."

Kylo stood straighter as we walked up. "This her? The succubus?"

"My name's Ivy."

When she moved to pass by, Kylo stepped into her path.

"Look meathead, I've been dicked around by too many men to count in the last week, so unless you're in the mood to get an ass whooping by a girl half your size, get the hell out of my way."

A smirk formed on Kylo's lips, and he looked to me. I nodded. As he moved aside, Ivy shoved at his chest and stormed inside. He turned and stood beside me, laughing. "Man, I can see how she got you by the balls. She's a hellcat, isn't she?"

"You have no idea."

Brax and Blaze sat on opposite sides of the girls, rising to their feet as Ivy charged forward. She froze a couple of steps away, shocked to see them free of gags and seemingly comfortable. They sat side by side on a blanket, eating the snacks Brax had bought for everyone.

"Ivy!" they both called out as she came into view.

She dropped to her knees in front of Jade. "Are you okay?" she asked, holding her sister's chin.

"Yes." Jade glanced to Violet beside her. "We're fine."

"Good. Have they done anything to you? Hurt you?"

Violet tossed a potato chip into her mouth. "Besides acting like bossy assholes? No. What about you? Are you all right?"

Ivy smiled, but underneath a sadness lingered. "You don't need to worry about me."

"Ivy." I tapped a finger to my watch.

She nodded and stood again. "All right. I'll be back later. I need to handle a few things first."

"You're not staying?" Jade asked

"Not today." Ivy looked to me. "There's something I need to do first." She hugged her sisters and followed me back outside into the evening desert heat, close enough to Brax and the crew, but far enough away as to give us some privacy.

"You said Bastian didn't have to know. What did you mean?"

I ran a hand down my jaw. "Brax created an illusion. It will hold up for a short amount of time, during which we—or you—need to obtain the vial. Bastian won't know you're working with me."

"What happens after I get you your blood?"

"Our business is done."

She glanced toward the ground and nodded only once. A sharp tinge of disappointment shot straight into my chest. I still wanted her. Even after everything, the pull I'd experienced toward Ivy since the very first night we met, remained.

"Bastian is strong. Stronger than you realize. If he finds out—

"He won't."

"How can he not? And how are we going to explain a bunch of dead ghouls and my sisters missing from where he left them? Or what about your suddenly missing blood?" She laughed. "I am so screwed."

"No, you're not."

A doubtful smile widened her luscious lips. "Oh yeah? How do you figure that?"

"I'll keep up the illusion. You go to Bastian's, grab my blood, and leave. Then we put your sisters back. The guys will raise hell and make a big scene drawing Bastian to the ghoul's place. By the time Bastian arrives, they'll be long gone."

"And what about the missing blood? We don't even know if it's still there. He may have already done something with it."

"No." I shook my head. "I would've known. Blood holds powerful magick, Ivy. Much greater than you can imagine."

In the short time I'd known her, I hadn't seen her this off her game. The pathetic pussy in me wanted to ease her worries. "We've got it covered. You're just going to have to trust me. None of this will come back to you."

She eyed me cautiously. "You're certain this illusion will hold?"

"As long as he doesn't pay them another in-person visit, we're fine."

"What do you need from me?"

Besides naked in my bed? I stuffed my hands into the pockets of my now uncomfortably tight pants. "Where is Bastian now?"

"Out of town. I don't know where, but he's not coming back until Saturday."

"Good. Then you've got between now and then to end this."

She swept the hair from her eyes and watched a shooting star skim across the sky overhead. "If this goes badly . . . if I get caught . . . I want your word that you'll release my sisters."

I closed some of the distance between us and she dropped her gaze to my advancing form. She moved back an inch, trying to reopen it.

"I won't let it go badly," I said.

Her nose scrunched up. "It's kind of hard to believe the man who's kidnapped my sisters and threatened their lives."

"It's in my best interest to keep you safe—at least until I get my vial." I lowered my head, until we were eye to eye. "So until then, I won't let you get hurt."

"I don't need a hero, Dante. I've been doing this on my own for years."

Crazy and thoroughly stupid, I couldn't stop myself from this uncontrollable desire for her. I closed the final gap. She didn't pull back, didn't flinch.

I saw it then. The hungry lust in her eyes masked behind fury. She still wanted me. It had never left. It was just lying in wait until she could force herself to forget it.

She raised her chin defiantly. "What?"

For a moment, I forgot about everything between us. All the rage. All the anger and confusion. I looked in her dark eyes and saw myself fall completely this time, only to land hard on my ass.

My lips hovered inches from hers.

Just when I thought she'd given in, she looked up into my eyes, and took a step back, her gaze steely and hardened.

I crossed my arms in front me, fighting the urge to grab her and pull her in for a kiss. Until she was sure of her sisters' safety, she would lean on the side of hating me.

"You're a sick bastard if you think I'd let you touch me again."

Always the queen of torment.

"I've been called worse, sweetheart."

"Stop calling me that."

"Whatever you say."

She spun around and stormed back down to the dirt road. I watched her form fade into the night, guilt flooding my senses. I wanted to call out to her. Make her stay.

"So she agreed, I take it?" Brax asked, appearing at my side seconds after Ivy left.

I nodded.

"Good. Do we know what was stolen?"

"Yes."

"Well?" he pressed.

"A vial of my blood."

He stood statuesque, thoughts flittered behind his eyes rapidly. "Why?"

"I don't know. But it's troubling. Something isn't right." A memory of something ominous stirred in my gut. "I'm worried what this will all turn out to be if I don't get it back."

"I'll hit the books. See what I can find."

"Thanks."

I watched the last spot where Ivy stood before fully disappearing from sight. I wanted to go after her. To end this before she or anyone else I cared about was in danger, but I fought my desire.

I knew I was drawn to her in the beginning, infatuated even. She was beautiful, smart, sassy, and strong. How could I not be? But to have feelings for her?

Shit. I tried to focus on disconnecting them, but instead, I kept thinking about her plump lips and how they tasted.

I looked at the campsite and then started walking. I needed to clear my head. Solitude would be the only way I could ever manage it successfully. I took off first walking then finally, worked myself into a run, letting my demon speed take over. I moved faster than humanly possible, convinced that I could outrun the mess that had clouded my mind—and hopefully come back with answers.

CHAPTER 14

Ivy

I wasn't looking forward to the eerie quiet back at the house. In all our years together, I'd never spent more than a few days without my sisters. It had never seemed too big until now, when it was suddenly the emptiest, loneliest home imaginable.

As I pulled into the lot, I saw Marla, fist raised, in front of my door.

Could this night get any worse?

In spite of my exhaustion, I jumped out of the car and jogged up to her. Whatever she had to say, I was sure it wasn't something I wanted to hear. But it was better to rip the bandage off now.

"Oh!" She turned and smiled at me, but it soon faded. "Ivy. I was about to say I'm glad I caught you, but . . . are you okay? You look pale."

"I'm fine," I insisted. "Just a little under the weather. Work was a bitch."

Marla nodded in understanding. "Well—I wish I had better news, but Bastian's returning in the morning. He wants you brought over tonight."

Shit.

"Didn't he just leave?"

She shrugged. "Yes, but plans changed and the trip got cut short."

Double shit. Did he know? It took everything in me to remain calm and keep my hands from shaking. "Is everything okay?"

"Oh, yes." She smiled, and her tone lightened. "It's fine, he just—you know—wants to see you. For . . . you know . . ."

"Oh."

In the midst of dealing with Dante, my mother, and my kidnapped sisters, I had actually forgotten about our stupid deal. The last thing I wanted to deal with right now was Bastian and his boner.

"Okay," said Marla, after I'd been standing there in silence too long. "Come on. Let's get you inside, and I'll put some water on. You need a cup of tea."

I wanted to protest, but I did hate the idea of being alone right now.

I sat down heavily on the sofa, trying not to think about how Jade would always sprawl here. I never usually sat here. There was never room.

"Did you get a read off of the imp?" she asked from across the kitchen, her hands busy filling my teapot.

"No, he never showed." Well—technically he could've showed when I was back in the office dry humping Dante, but Marla didn't need to know that.

"Hmmm, interesting."

Shit. I hoped that wouldn't come back to bite me in the ass. "Is Bastian going to be pissed?"

"About the imp?" She grabbed a mug from the cabinet, her back to me. "He shouldn't be. It was a tipoff, but he could've gotten wind we were looking for him and decided to hightail back out of town." She raised the box of Chamomile tea in one hand and Lemon Balm in the other, reading the backs of each. "I'd normally say chamomile, but lemon balm's supposed to be great for the nervous system." She chuckled. "Well—in humans at least."

"Marla?"

She looked up, her catlike eyes fixed on me.

"I can't go to his place tonight," I heard myself say numbly. "I'm sorry, I don't want to get anyone in trouble, least of all you . . . but I just can't."

Marla stood there for a second, looking at me searchingly. Then she nodded. "I get it, hon. Believe me. I understand. I'll postpone, okay? Don't worry, just leave it to me."

She pulled out her phone and tucked it between her ear and shoulder while she dug out a kettle and put some water on to boil.

I hadn't let anyone take care of me in a long time. It's . . . strange. Discomfiting. But nice—in a really weird way.

". . . yes, found her . . . but listen . . . she's not feeling well, I'm afraid. . . What? . . . Oh no, nothing serious. A touch of you know, women's troubles. I knew you'd understand."

Before I knew it, she'd appeared in front of me with a teacup that I didn't even know we owned.

"Thank you," I said, maybe a little too fervently. I realized my voice shook. And my hands. And my everything.

"Are you sure you're all right?" Marla asked, perching on the old coffee table across from me.

"I don't know," I confessed. "I don't know much of anything right now."

I had forgotten how simple life seemed before Bastian sent me to Reno. Before I met Dante. Before my sisters were kidnapped.

Tears pricked at my eyes, threatening to fall. I knew I could trust Marla, but I still didn't want her to see me cry. I didn't like anyone to see me cry.

"Drink your tea," she said gently. "Everything seems a lot clearer after a nice hot cup. Trust me."

"I'm more of a beer girl," I confessed. "But this is nice."

And it was. Sort of mild and sweet and calming. I hadn't thought to ask her which type of tea it was. Obviously, something herbal, that's all we ever bought. As the warm liquid swirled in my belly, I started to feel the creeping edges of exhaustion that I'd been putting off for so long.

"Here," Marla said, appearing with the old afghan off the broken recliner. "Lie down. You look like you could use a good rest."

She was right, and, anyway, I didn't have the energy to protest. Sure, Bastian's unplanned early return would complicate things, but I couldn't deal with it right now. I'd face the shitstorm tomorrow.

The last thing I saw before my heavy lids fell was Marla picking up my teacup from the table and holding it while she watched me drift off. A few moments later, I heard her carry it out to the kitchen.

So this is what it was like to have a mom.

CHAPTER 15

DANTE

"I hope you're not planning on using that."

Brax's squinted eyes slid over to the crossbow I was restringing. His hand raised to cover the sunlight as he tried to hide his uncertainty. He hadn't succeeded.

"I haven't decided yet." I grunted and tossed him a fresh clip of silver bullets.

Jade and Violet's anxious energy permeated through the air like a poisonous gas. They'd kept up the appearance of casual indifference, at least Violet did, but Jade was more like a baby rabbit left in the burrow, wondering if Momma was ever coming home. For all her efforts, Violet's back stood a little too straight, her eyes a little too glassy. She forced a smile every time Jade shot her one of those scared, unsure looks.

When she caught me watching, she slammed her thermos down and gave me her back. The temper on these women. Violet didn't have quite the same attitude as Ivy, but she was getting damn close. Too close for comfort. The last thing I needed was two of her chewing on my ear.

Tires squealed in the distance, then a door slammed, and heavy footfalls crunched over gravel from the bottom of the hill.

Ivy. Just like she read my mind. Maybe she did.

The sound caught Violet's attention, and she left Brax, who'd taken up the role of her personal supervisor, running over to meet her sister.

In all the years I'd known Brax, he'd never stopped to watch a beautiful woman, for more than a minute—max. With Violet, he studied everything. Noticed everything. Though she likely hadn't realized it, I did. Brax 's interest in Violet went beyond temporary caretaker.

"I don't know what's worse. With the gags or without," he muttered, scratching the back of his neck as both girls ran to meet Ivy.

"You're the one who wanted to stop treating them like fugitives," I pointed out. "This is what happens. Start talking to them like human beings, and they start acting like it. Wanting answers."

Ivy, having gently shaken off her sisters, advanced toward us before I knew it. Shit, what kind of super-speed powers did these girls have?

"What would you know about treating anyone like a human being, Dante?" she asked, and Brax quickly retreated. Apparently, dealing with Violet was the lesser of two evils.

"That's funny," I muttered, picking up my crossbow again, "coming from you."

"What's this?" She gestured vaguely at the arsenal I had laid out.

"These . . ." I waved a hand over them, ". . . are called wea . . . pons." I said the last word slowly.

"No shit, Sherlock." She ran a finger down the long blade and I tensed, hand ready on the bow in case she came for me. "No need for the smartass response."

"If you don't want a smartass answer, don't ask dumbass questions."

She bit down on the inside of her full bottom lip and crossed her arms. Like I said, tempers. "Look, I came here to tell you, the plans have changed."

"You're really gonna try to go back on this? Trust me when I say that I'm an enemy you don't want to cross."

My pride took the biggest hit when she acted as though Bastian could best me. She acted like he was the ultimate badass, and I couldn't match him.

She was wrong.

Ivy sighed. "Did I say anything about backing out?"

"You sucked my soul out. Why can't you do the same to Bastian? Too afraid?" I asked, louder than I really had to.

Both of Ivy's sisters jerked their heads up. I ignored them.

"Hey." Ivy grabbed my arm, and I let her drag me a few feet away. "Keep it down, okay? I don't need my sisters knowing all the gory details about . . . my situation."

I stared at her. "They don't know what you are?"

She'd flushed bright red, all the way down her chest. "It's not exactly something I discuss with them on the regular, no. So, stop being a dick."

I let out a bark of laughter. "A bashful succubus. Never thought I'd see the day."

"I'm not a . . ." She had to force herself to spit it out. "Succubus. I'm a human being."

"Sure, you are, sweetheart." I sat down on a stump and continued working on my crossbow. "You know, I spent a couple hundred years denying what I was, too. Easier that way, at first. But you can't run forever. Embrace it. You're gonna need your powers to steal my blood back from this bastard, anyway. Now's not the time to get all shifty about it."

Arms crossed, she sighed heavily, shifting her weight from one foot to the other. "Bastian's back."

I snapped my head up. "You said Saturday. Why's he back now?"

"I don't know, but his assistant came by last night, she tried to get me to go over there."

"Does he know?" I asked.

She rubbed a hand down her bare arms. "I don't think so."

"You said you got out of it. How?"

"I delayed it—I didn't get out of it." She crouched down onto her knee. "I think I can still get it, but I'm going to have to do things differently."

I quirked a brow. "Differently?" An unpleasant thought occurred to me. I set the bow aside and looked up. "You're planning on seducing him."

She nodded tersely.

I swallowed down the violent rage stirring my tattoos to life. Ivy was going to seduce Bastian. Possibly screw him, just to get back my blood.

"How? I thought he controls your powers?"

"He doesn't control me," Ivy snapped, even as her eyes widened defensively. "The reason he made me, made my sisters, is because he can't do what I do. He doesn't control it. He doesn't even really understand it."

"That may be." I got to my feet, closing the short distance between us. "But he's going to be at least as resistant to you as I am, right? Now that I know what you are. What you did." I still got a little sick, a little lightheaded, thinking about it. Her inside my mind, crawling around in my brain like a parasite. Now she'd be crawling around in Bastian—and him in her.

"Maybe," she admitted, chewing on her lower lip. I fought to ignore the flare of lust that simple tic brought up in my groin. It's all a trick. It's just a trick.

"We have to assume that," I insisted. "Prepare for the worst. That glamour of yours is a handy thing to have, but no matter how hot Bastian is for you . . ., " I let the rising anger in my throat ebb down, " . . . he's gonna know something is up, unless you really bring out the big guns."

"Fine," she agreed. "Yes. You're right."

"So, you'd better practice," I heard myself say. "And I only know one guy who can resist you well enough to build your succubus-muscles."

What the hell are you doing? Why the hell are you inviting her back into your brain, after what she did?

Ignoring the sensible voice in my head, I stood my ground.

Ivy was already shaking her head. "No way."

"That's it? Just no?" I glared at her.

"No is a complete sentence," she replied. "No. That's it. I'm not playing these games with you."

"They're not games," I told her, shifting my eyes over to her sisters. It was a subtle reminder, but it was all she needed. I still had sway over her. Badass as she tried to act, I could still snap her neck without breaking a sweat. And then there'd be no one left to protect her little sisters.

"This isn't going to help," she insisted. "And it's just going to wear you out."

"You let me worry about that," I grunted. "Come on. You don't want your sisters to see this, do you?"

"See what?" she demanded as I started walking into the forest. "I don't even know what you want me to do."

"You'll figure it out," I replied with a dry smirk. "I believe in you."

Running after me, she panted out a few more halfhearted objections, but she couldn't keep up with the length of my stride and the energy of her outrage at the same time. So much for those super-speed powers.

When we reached another clearing, I stopped abruptly, and she almost crashed into me.

"Feels like you should've seen that coming," I deadpanned.

She glared at me.

"So, you've never used your powers on him before?" I asked.

Ivy shook her head. "I don't see the point . . ."

I silenced her with a raised finger. "But he knows what you can do. He'll be on guard."

"Not exactly," she said hesitantly. Her eyes slipped away from my gaze. "We kind of . . ."

"Go on," I prompted her.

"He's kind of expecting me," she said finally, "to show up at his place. To let him, uh . . . to give him a chance to . . ."

She blushed. What exactly had she promised him? I didn't like the sound of it.

Jealousy churned in my gut. I had no right to feel it, but the green monster didn't care.

"To screw you?"

"Seduce me," she muttered at last.

I almost laughed out loud. This Bastian character sure was high on his own seductiveness, wasn't he? Did he really think he could entice a succubus? How?

Judging by Ivy's expression and the way she dug her toe of her sneaker into the grass, she wasn't confident in her ability.

All the more reason to do this.

Before I could think better of it, I reached out and grabbed her chin. She flinched, but didn't try to pull away.

"Ivy, look at me. You're more powerful than he is," I told her. "You said it yourself, right? He doesn't understand what you can do. He's full of himself. He thinks he owns you. He doesn't. You can go in there, let him believe he's got sway over you, but he doesn't. You've got the upper hand. Not just because of your powers. Not just because of who you are. What you are. You've got the upper hand because he wants you. More than you want him."

My throat went dry. I swallowed hard. If she caught that I wasn't just talking about Bastian anymore, she didn't show it.

"Fine," she said softly. "I'm going to try to get into your head now. Get ready."

She reached out and grabbed my arm. Slowly, I let go of her face. I wasn't sure if the extra skin contact helped or not. But I wasn't going to give her anything to make it easier.

"Look at me," she said. I met her eyes.

Instantly, I was slammed with memories of the night in the casino. The second she saw me, she had that look. I thought it was just her. But it wasn't her—at least, not the Ivy I'd known since then. It was her succubus side. It was her glamour.

But now, I knew what it was. I knew the tendrils in my brain weren't from cheap whiskey. I knew my chest constricted with magic, not loneliness. My heart pounded, and I focused on steadying my breaths. I couldn't control everything, but I could control that.

I pictured a wall. Strong, tall, impenetrable. As far as the eye could see. Disappearing into the horizon. In front of me, nothing but smooth stone rose. My vision was gray. In my mind's eye, I rested a palm on the wall. Steady. Secure. Safe.

Ivy's Mona Lisa smile started to quiver. Her eye twitched slightly, and in the distance, something enticing drifted over the wall I'd built. Something delicious and perfect. Honeysuckle and lavender.

I inhaled, but I wouldn't budge. The wall was still sturdy and real in my head, and I forced myself to imagine the scraping of stone against the pads of my fingers. Anything to hold onto my security.

Ivy nibbled her lip, but I barely saw it. Even though I hadn't broken eye contact, I had somehow broken her spell. My chest swelled with pride. But I didn't show it.

I stood there, steady and unmoving, just like my wall.

Suddenly Ivy gasped, groaned, pitching forward and almost collapsing against me. I caught her, shaking myself back to reality. It might have been a trick. But it wasn't. Her glamour was broken. I could feel it disappear like cobwebs in the wind.

Almost angrily, she pushed herself away from me and stood on shaking legs. "What was that, Dante?" she demanded.

"Child's play," I replied. I was exhausted, too, but I did a better job of hiding it. You didn't last long in my job if you let 'em see you bleed.

"Screw you," she huffed, swiping her sleeve across her forehead. "Bastian's not going to come on that strong. He has no idea what to expect. I'll have him eating out of my hand before he knows what's going on."

"So you say," I replied, gruffly. "I hope you're right, because that was—"

"Pathetic," she said, before I could think of a softer word. "I get it. So, are you gonna let me try again?"

"Catch your breath first," I told her.

"I'm ready," she insisted. "Build your wall, asshole. I'm coming with a wrecking ball."

And then she came at me full-force, not gentle tendrils anymore. No, this was something feral, squeezing around my mind and heart so fast it almost knocked the wind out of me.

I shoved back mentally with all the strength I could muster. Without moving, I pushed at her magic. But my psychic wall wasn't gonna do me much good now. She was was already inside my head.

A black cloud of anger surrounded my mind's eye as I fought her for control. The dark succubus side of Ivy's magic didn't like being thwarted. The mist slowly morphed into several more tentacles, groping blindly for me in our mental battle.

I dodged. Coughing up smoke in this world or the real one, who knew? And who was to say which one was real, anyway? I struggled against her, ignoring the strange pleasure her touch brought. If I closed my eyes, it was like the warmest, sweetest embrace I'd ever known.

It wasn't just sexual. It was everything. All of me, body and soul, wanted to give in. Ached. I was desperate for more, even as I panicked, even as I drowned.

The real world was starting to fade around me. Shit. No. If I didn't keep at least one foot rooted in reality, I'd lose this fight for sure. It seemed impossible, fracturing my mind in two. One half of me just focused on standing upright in the sunny meadow, keeping my eyes open, blinking, breathing. The other half, fighting for my life against a goddamn sea demon from the depths of a watery hell.

Because, yeah, I was at sea. Somehow, she was even controlling the environment, and we pitched and rocked in a leaking boat. How did she know this would put me on edge? Where did she catch on that slippery wood and the smell of brine would make me panic, make me seek out the comfort of her embrace even more?

Shit, she was good. But I was better.

I'd almost forgotten the most important part. By digging this deep into my mind, she'd left open channels of herself, too. I delved in, slipping free of her grasp just enough to find the crack she'd left open.

At first, she didn't notice. She thought I was surrendering. That moment of triumph, just a little distraction, was all I needed.

Suddenly, I was wading in memories. The shoreline of her subconscious was laid out all around me. It was almost too easy. I saw the form of a man, her father maybe, or no—no, that was too dark a memory, too angry. The bitterness would push her too far back. I kept on searching. I needed something that ran deep, but not too deep. Something she was afraid of. Something she wouldn't be expecting.

And there it was. Lurking in her memories, a small Ivy, frozen with fear in a rundown backyard. Late at night. Nobody home. Just Ivy and the baby—Violet I guessed. Momma was out again, and Daddy, well, Daddy was never home.

Ivy stared at the wolf, and the wolf stared back.

It must've hopped over the fence, looking for food. Maybe chasing some prey. It was an ordinary wolf, I thought, but in the memories of Little Ivy, it was a massive thing with yellow eyes and snarling jaws.

Good enough.

I stepped into its skin like a secondhand coat. Advancing on Little Ivy, I growled, letting the drool run from my massive teeth.

Instantly, reality cracked around us. I was fracturing the connection. Ivy created this world, and her fear was going to destroy it.

The boat capsized, the tentacles shriveled and fell away. I had regained control of my universe. My own mind. It belonged to me again.

Little Ivy let out a piercing shriek, and I threw my head back and howled in response.

Jolted back to the real world, I fell to my knees—head pounding, eyes burning, lungs aching. It had taken every bit of my energy to fight her off. To regain control.

Ivy slumped on the grass in front of me, pale as death, unmoving. I held back my panic long enough to watch her chest for a subtle rise and fall.

Yes, she was still breathing. It was shallow, but it was there. I reached out and shook her awake.

For a second, she stared at me, dazed. Then the outrage came.

"What the hell was that?" she demanded, her voice shaking and slightly hoarse. "I didn't . . . you weren't . . . that wasn't . . ."

"I'm not going easy on you," I replied. "Neither will he."

"Hey, guys?" Brax's voice, faint but recognizable, cut through the trees to the clearing. "Everyone decent?"

Ivy swore under her breath, struggling to her feet. I almost offered her a hand but then thought better of it.

"Yes," I yelled. "We're training."

"Uh-huh," said Brax, jogging closer, his eyes going over our sweat-covered skin. "I've been reading over some of the books I found and . . ." He glanced to Ivy and then me, silently asking if I wanted him to continue in her presence. I nodded.

"Look, it'll be easier to explain if I can refer back to them. Come on."

Groaning softly, I started the trek back to the fire pit.

Why couldn't it wait? My demon wanted to punch Brax for barging in, but I've never met a single necromancer that worked better after being decked by a demon in the throat.

Ivy shuffled behind me, drained but still walking. I was impressed. I'd managed to knock her out cold with my counterattack, but she was already back on her feet.

"You don't fight fair," she muttered as we made our way through the trees.

"No such thing," I replied. "Remember who we're dealing with."

"He's not as bad as you think."

I bit my tongue.

"All right, all right," Brax called out as we neared the camp. He had one book opened in each hand, like he was about to give the world's worst sermon. "Listen. Dante, I know you've never been a big fan of the half-breed prophecy—"

I turned around and started to retreat.

"Wait, wait!" Brax ran after me. "I swear to the gods, Dante, you gotta listen to me. Just this once. Okay? There are too many damn coincidences here, and I don't like it. We need to figure out what's really going on."

"I know what's really going on," I growled. "Ivy stole a vial of my blood to give to her demon-sire because he wants to create some fucked up Frankenstein version of me."

"Reverse engineer your DNA." Brax nodded.

I looked to Ivy. "Correct?"

She leaned back, a snarky grin on her face. "Just so I'm clear. Are we all on the same team now? Sharing information, etcetera? Because if that's the case, I want my sisters freed."

Again with the ridiculous negotiations.

"No, you're on my team, doing as I say. And I expect you to answer —honestly."

She turned to Brax. "Maybe, that's what he does? That's kind of Bastian's thing?"

Brax went on. "And that's where it gets even weirder. Ivy, your connection with Bastian—how deep does it run, exactly?"

"I don't know," Ivy replied, rubbing her temples. "I mean, he can send out these pulses, these . . . migraines, seizures, I don't know. If I try to directly go against his orders, he can knock me down for the count. It's like some psychic collar. But it only goes so far. And he can't read my mind. Just like I can't read his, not really. I'd have to dig deep. Use my powers on him. And I've never done that."

"Right," Brax said. "Well, do you trust him?"

"Not as far as I can throw him," she replied dryly. "Why? Do you think he's got something sinister planned? I mean, more sinister than creating a Frankenstein/demon/half-breed army out of bits of blood and teeth?"

Brax inhaled sharply. "You tell me."

He held up one of the dusty old books, spreading the pages open for us to examine. There was an intricate drawing spanning them, showing a massive demon with curling horns and a mile-wide wingspan. Underneath his feet the earth cracked, showing the fires of Hell beneath.

"I'm not getting the connection," Ivy murmured.

"This is . . . well, let's call him Fred." Brax tapped the drawing. "He has another name, but it can't really be pronounced in English or most other languages. Fred's always been somewhat of a mystery. He's tied to the lore about the Apocalypse, you know, the end of the human world as we know it. When the age of man ends, and the age of demons begins."

Jade and Violet sat by in rapt attention. I wanted to roll my eyes and walk away, but, much as I hated to admit it, Brax actually had my attention. For all we'd talked about this stupid half-breed prophecy, he'd never tied it into the legends of the world-ending demon before.

"Sure," Ivy said. "Good old Fred. I think we went to high school together."

"Here's the thing." Brax flipped a few pages in the book. "Right here, there's a reference to the rise of Fred in conjunction with a particular syzygy." He glanced around, waiting for someone to catch on. "That's, uh, that's a Greek word. It refers to a specific lineup of three heavenly bodies. Even back when these books were written, people had the ability to accurately predict coming eclipses, et cetera, et cetera. They knew about the solar eclipse coming next month. When that happens, Mercury, Earth, and our sun will be in perfect alignment."

"Perfect alignment for what?" Ivy asked.

Brax wagged his finger at her. "Great question. I had the exact same thought, because, like, why? We've had tons of eclipses, tons of different celestial alignments. What was so special about this one? And how was it gonna give rise to a special world-ending demon, right? It doesn't make any sense."

"Sure," I cut in finally. "Unlike the usual prophecies."

"I'm getting to the interesting part," he promised me with a hint of a grin. "Okay. I shouldn't make light of it. This is actually some serious shit. But, man, it's exciting to have found something concrete for once. Okay." He took a deep breath and adjusted his glasses. "I started pouring over the demonic lore for some other reference to this particular syzygy."

"You've gotta stop saying that," I warned him. "The urge to punch you gets stronger every time. Almost like it's some magical spell."

Kylo and Damon snickered, but Brax ignored me.

"And I found something else. A recipe. I couldn't tell you if it was for a spell or a potion or what. Not at first. A lot of it was abbreviated or written in code." He opened another book and pointed to a long, scrawling list of mostly unintelligible symbols and ancient lettering.

"Yeah, no kidding," Ivy muttered.

"Thankfully, I was able to read a little bit deeper into it than most people," Brax said, a spark in his eyes. "With my vision, I could see what was in the minds and hearts of those who wrote it. And, you know . . . I kind of wish I hadn't looked. It wasn't pretty. At first, I couldn't make sense of it. It was dark. A lot of pain, a lot of suffering. Fire and brimstone. I finally saw the important part of the vision. It was only a glimpse, but it was enough."

He jerked his head toward the drawing of Fred, still propped open against his knee.

Ivy glanced from the drawing to his face and then back again a few times.

"Are you saying this . . . this potion, this ritual, whatever? It has something to do with bringing Fred to manifest?"

Brax nodded. "I think so. The thing is, usually a demon is summoned. It's a very specific kind of ritual, and it's easy enough to recognize. A few candles, a sigil, maybe a dash of human sacrifice. But nothing like this. This is something different and altogether darker. It's a recipe. It's building instructions."

"So, you're saying, this Fred . . . " Ivy exhaled softly. "He doesn't actually exist? He's not a demon that can be summoned; he's a creature that has to be made?"

Brax nodded slowly. "I know it sounds crazy. More than the usual spells and prophecies. But I was able to translate a little of the recipe, with a lot of research and a lot of brute force codebreaking. I should work for the damn CIA."

Violet stared at him. Angry, snarky and irritated—but underneath it all, intrigued. As though she'd just seen him for the first time. Ivy was not gonna like that.

"And that's where I noticed something," Brax went on. "One of the crucial ingredients in this ritual, this recipe, is a vial of blood drawn out of the heart vein from the half breed of the prophecy."

If we were sitting at a table, I would've flipped it.

My tattoos seared against my flesh, the edges creating a steady pulse of fiery pain. My demon roared.

"No." I stood abruptly. Kylo and Damon positioned themselves between me and the women, while everyone else who gathered around Brax like faithful disciples, jumped.

Blaze said, "The fuck, Dante?"

"This stupid goddamn prophecy," I growled, staring Brax down. His steady gaze didn't waver. "You keep on beating this drum. I'm telling you it's just a bunch of stupid coincidences. I'm not part of some greater plan."

The four men looked at each other but didn't argue. Finally, after minutes of heavy silence, Brax nodded.

"Fair enough," he said quietly. "You're the boss."

"That's right, I am." I marched across the campsite, snagging a beer out of the ice chest Kylo had picked up, and flipped off the cap, downing the entire bottle in one swig. Right now, I wished it were Fae wine and not this cheap human bullshit.

From the corner of my eye, I watched Ivy hugging her sisters as if she was getting ready to leave. 'Ivy training' drained me more than I cared to admit, but I still needed to do one more thing.

"Ivy," I called as I walked passed her, heading farther away from the group.

She dropped her arms from around Jade. "What?"

I stopped and crooked a finger at her. "Follow me. Now."

CHAPTER 16

Ivy

I swallowed. Shit. What did he want?

"Why?"

His lips couldn't have flattened any further. "Do you ever stop asking questions?"

Reluctant as my steps were, I followed after him, beyond the cover of a large oak tree.

"What do you want, Dante?"

"It's not what I want," he said, almost humoring me with his sudden ability to look out for someone other than himself. "It's what you need."

"What I—" My breath caught in my throat. He didn't need to explain any further, not as his arms lifted and pinned me between him and the tree at my back. "No Dante, just . . . no."

I may have welcomed more energy and strength, but I wasn't oblivious to how it drained others. It also drew me further toward him. And who was to say he wouldn't need it more than me?

"Ivy, it'll be fine." He sounded so certain I nearly believed him.

"Look, you can't be—"

His finger pressed across my lips, the heat of him nearly more convincing than his words.

"It will be fine," he reiterated, so solidly I couldn't find it in myself to refute him. No matter how angry or upset I was, that ever-present pull remained.

"Okay," I breathed, as I ignored my sense of loss at his dropped finger. "Fine." At least this would be me taking from him, rather than the other way around.

His hands settled back against the tree, leaving me wondering if it was his warmth or mine that seemed to fill the space between us. Already I could smell his heady scent, covered with a small dose of the beer he'd just downed. And I could almost taste the vigor he was so apt to freely give.

My rational mind screamed how bad this idea was, but I couldn't fight it—fight her. My succubus always claimed her heart's desires, even when I tried to stop her.

With a single, sliding step forward I closed the gap between us and breathed in his strength. I'd barely even pulled, yet his energy flowed into me like a river, intoxicating me in seconds. My lashes fluttered upward, their lack of stillness born of the stupor that had me staring into Dante's determined, yet lustful gaze.

I didn't want to see that look in his eyes, not as the strength of his energy surged through me and left me panting in desire. Yet, some things just aren't worth fighting.

The collar of his shirt curled into my grip, and I pulled him down until our lips crashed in a fit of lust as he shoved me back against the tree. Knots and snapped-off branches dug into my back, but the pain was easy to ignore as I kissed him with more fury than ever before.

He was feeding me—my energy and my lust—and with my hands snaking down his chest, I wasn't sure I'd ever find an escape. His tongue trailed across my lips opening floodgates even I could not have predicted. His energy was strong, but the swells of energy crashing over me then were unlike anything I'd ever felt.

My limbs tingled in a strange exhilaration as I deepened the kiss and pulled . . . and pulled.

A whisper of warning tugged at the back of my mind and went on ignored second after intoxicating second. Yet, the tick of it was like a fly buzzing in one's ear, and soon, I could silence it no more.

As empty as it made me feel, I pushed upon Dante's chest, freeing myself of not only the taste of his lips, but the surging power of his energy. I could still feel it, as if it pulsated through my veins, while the dampness of my lips had my tongue sweeping out in taste of it.

"Thanks." It was the best I could offer as I forced myself to slip away from his grasp and the magnetism that threatened to drag me back.

A day had passed since Brax's little campfire lesson. Tonight, I'd head for Bastian's, seduce him, subdue him, grab the vial, and wait for the place to be attacked.

I still didn't know what to make of Brax's theories. Dante was resistant to them, and I didn't want to bring them up again. As for Bastian's part in it—well, he was definitely a bit crazy, but was he the right kind of crazy to try to create a world-ending demonic Frankenstein's monster?

I doubted it. He'd always talked about how much he liked living here between worlds, surrounded by humans, experimenting on how best to meld their natural abilities with those of demons and other nonhuman beings. He wasn't really an apocalypse type of guy.

Maybe if he'd misread something or misunderstood an old recipe. But I'd looked through his library before. There was nothing in it like what Brax had shown us. I didn't believe he could hide something of that magnitude.

But, then, why blood from the heart-vein? Why wouldn't any blood or skin cells do? Why was he so specific? Just because it was easy to collect? It did seem like a hell of a coincidence.

Of course, there was another possibility at play. Bastian had always loomed so large in my life: my creator, sire, alpha, and omega. No matter how much I wanted to deny it, he surrounded my life, and his desires and plans permeated every decision I made. But he wasn't that powerful. In the grand scheme of things, he was just one of many magical beings who pulled strings beyond strings that I couldn't even imagine.

Was it possible, after all this time, that Bastian was really in someone else's pocket? Without even realizing it himself?

Could Bastian just be a pawn in a much bigger game?

It was a troubling thought, one that wouldn't leave me alone as I dressed and curled my hair for the night's . . . festivities. I already knew exactly how to dress and act if I wanted to get Bastian's attention and keep it. It was just a matter of guarding my mind from the exploit Dante had used because if Bastian could read my thoughts as easily as Dante did, well, we were all doomed.

And if he was being played by someone much more powerful . . . I had to focus on getting this done, one step at a time.

Get the vial back. Give it to Dante. Get my sisters to safety.

If you still could. Gods I hoped Bastian hadn't already used it. I couldn't face the consequences that would bring on my sisters and me or the rest of the world.

I didn't want to believe Dante would hurt them. I was almost certain he wouldn't. He had a right to be pissed off, to ask this of me.

The rumble of engines outside my window alerted me that Dante and his boys were ready for action. I wasn't sure how he planned on approaching the compound without letting the guards know what was up, but I'd left that part of the planning to him. It was a show of trust I was now beginning to regret.

My hooker heels weren't exactly made for hiking.

I walked out onto the driveway, just as dusk fell. Dante straddled his bike, the engine idling. His eyes penetrated mine even before he lifted the face shield of his helmet.

Did he even need a damn helmet? What's the worst that could happen to a creature like him in an accident?

Blaze wolf-whistled, but Dante cut him off with a sharp gesture. "Can you ride in that?" He made a vague gesture at my dress.

I hiked up the skirt, letting the high slit do its job and free enough of my legs to straddle the bike and wrap my arms around Dante's muscular bulk.

I could feel everyone's eyes on me, but I was too focused and amped on tonight's plan to worry about it.

We'd gone over the details so many times, but my mind still raced with anxiety. And I couldn't stop thinking about what Brax told us. What if he was right? What if we were walking into something bigger than all of us, something we weren't equipped to handle? Shit, none of us were the real-life heroes.

I wasn't sure what Dante had up his sleeve. His psychic resistance against my mental invasion was impressive. Maybe he still hid some of his powers or didn't fully understand them himself. Much as I hated to admit it, I was grateful to him for teaching me about my own weaknesses. I would be much more careful with Bastian.

Before I knew it, the bikes growled to a stop. We weren't too far from Bastian's mansion, close enough that I frowned with concern at the possibility of us being heard. I hopped off the bike before he had a chance to kill the engine, straightening my dress as I waited for the rest of the pack to disembark.

"I guess you're not worried about being heard?" I asked.

"I whipped up a little spell for that," Brax piped up, pulling off his helmet. "None of his people are gonna hear a damn thing we don't want 'em to."

"Great," I said. "So . . ."

Dante rested his hands on my shoulders, looking down at me with a thousand emotions swirling in his eyes. It caught me off guard, and I swallowed thickly.

I was overtaken with the urge to kiss him.

"Are you ready?" he asked me softly.

I nodded. "Just like we talked about. Give me twenty minutes, and you'll have your run of the place."

Dante nodded shortly, glanced over his shoulder, then back at me. He lowered his voice even more. "Ivy . . ."

I blinked.

"I know what you have to do," he said, his voice gravelly and low. "But . . ."

I raised my eyebrows slightly. "Yeah?"

"Don't feel like . . . don't let him . . ." He sighed, shaking his head with frustration. "Don't let him take advantage of you, okay? Don't feel like you have to overdo it; don't compromise your integrity. I know how much influence you can have with just a kiss. There's no need . . ."

I laughed in spite of myself. "Are you telling me not to go too far? Dante, I'm going to do whatever I need to do. The time for moderation passed a while ago. Right about when you kidnapped my sisters."

A shadow passed over his expression. For a second, it looked like he was going to keep talking, but then he released me.

I stepped back, then away. He turned to his men, and I began my walk.

In order for our plan to work, I had to reach the house alone. This wouldn't arouse anyone's suspicion, even with me on foot and dressed like a high-class call girl. After all, this was Bastian's place, and tonight I was just another one of his girls.

My heartbeat quickened as I approached the house. There were twice as many guards posted around the entrance, and I suddenly wished I had a way to communicate with Dante. To warn him. But it didn't matter, of course. This part was on me.

I smiled at them as I swayed forward, focusing my energies on sending little tendrils of persuasion in their direction. At first, there was no reaction. Then I noticed one of them slump his shoulders slightly. Another's nostrils flared, as if he smelled something unexpected and delicious.

I've still got it.

I had to conserve the majority of my energy for Bastian, of course. But I was so much stronger since practicing with Dante. I had a greater control over my power, more like an invisible muscle, another limb I could pilot with finesse.

The guards nodded and murmured their greetings. I smiled, gliding past them and into the foyer.

The house was eerily empty. I knew it wouldn't be for long. If Bastian hadn't already sensed my presence, he would in a moment. I tried to keep thoughts of seduction and arousal at the forefront of my mind, just in case he could read more than I gave him credit for.

A moment later, I heard footsteps coming from one of the side hallways. But it wasn't Bastian's steady gait. It was smaller, more clipped. Marla.

She appeared as if by magic. "Oh." Stopping, head cocked slightly to the side, she regarded me like I was a display at the zoo. I'd never known that kind of emotion coming from her, and it briefly threw me off my guard. Was it . . . jealousy? But, surely, she knew this was coming.

I smiled at her, considering whether to waste any of my energies on her. There shouldn't be any need because there was absolutely no reason for her to interfere. But I had such a strange sense of . . . darkness, like she hid something.

But I didn't have any time to waste on this.

"I'm here to see Bastian," I told her. "You know. To fulfill our agreement."

"Of course," she said lightly, quickly regaining her poise. "Wait here. I'll go and fetch him."

"No need," came an all-too-familiar voice from the top of the grand spiral staircase.

Bastian took his time, hand gliding along the banister, but his eyes never left mine. I took a deep breath, sending my glamour out into the space between us, reaching for him, like one might caress a lover's cheek across a restaurant table.

"I'm so glad you're here," he purred as he drew closer to me. "But I thought I'd have a bit more warning."

"You don't like surprises?" I asked him, in the softest, sexiest, faux-innocent tone I could manage. He exhaled sharply. It was working.

"When they're as beautiful as you?" Bastian reached out and tugged lightly on one of the curled tendrils of hair framing my face. "I certainly won't complain."

"Good. That would certainly put a damper on things." I leaned my head toward the adjoining sitting room. "Can we have a drink, sir?"

"Oh. I do love it when you call me that." He grinned, tilting his arm toward me. I tucked my hand into the handle he provided and let him lead me. "Yes, let's have that drink. We've got all night, haven't we?"

"I certainly don't have any plans," I laughed lightly.

If he noticed my behavior was a little off, it certainly wasn't affecting his attitude toward me. Dante had been right. I had the upper hand here, thanks to his desire for me blinding his common sense.

Oh, and my succubus powers. Those were always useful.

I exerted my influence, slowly and carefully. I didn't want to put him on guard. So far, he was only receptive. There was no hint of resistance, not like with Dante. This might be easier than I imagined.

In the sitting room, Bastian snapped his fingers, bringing a blue-flamed fire to life in the fireplace across from the overstuffed red leather armchairs. Then he went to the liquor cart and gestured toward it, like he was presenting the prizes in a game show.

"What's your poison, doll?"

My smile froze. God, but I hated it when he called me that. It reminded me too much of what I was. Of what we were. I was just a puppet on a string.

Focus.

"I'll have whatever you're having," I purred.

He laughed, dark and indulgent. "Good girl. What's gotten into you tonight? So amenable."

Shit. Even if it was just an idle question, it betrayed that I wasn't acting like myself. Bastian wasn't stupid. I had to stop laying it on so thick.

I walked to him, laughing. "Maybe I'm just trying to throw you off your guard, so I can toss your favorite aged brandy in your face."

Tsking and shaking his head, he handed me a glass. "There's my Ivy. But I know you wouldn't dare. I treat you too well. Haven't I always?"

"Of course," I muttered into the rim of my glass. I took a tiny sip, just enough to keep up appearances. It burned my lips, and all the way down my throat.

"I know I don't say it often enough," he began, his eyes roving over my body with admiration that wavered uncomfortably between a lover's hunger and a father's pride. "But I really am proud of you. Everything you've become. You haven't even come close to hitting the zenith of your true powers, and you're already so . . ." He searched for the right word.

I saw all the rejected choices floating around his head. Useful. Handy. Serviceable.

"Impressive," he said finally.

"I'll drink to that." I smiled.

For a moment, his expression grew thoughtful. He glanced at the fire, and then briefly back at my face. "You know, Ivy, I want to thank you for giving me this chance. I know you don't have to. And it means . . . it means the world to me."

If I wasn't careful, I was going to end up sympathizing with the madman who cursed me to this life as a half-breed demon.

"I know what you're thinking," he went on. "I'm never lacking for companions to warm my bed. And that's true. But after a while, you get tired of the meaningless trysts. They don't care about me. They don't know me, not really. But you . . ." He smiled, sipping his drink. "Well, you know all the worst of me, I suppose. And that's a comfort."

I reached out and touched his arm, channeling another rush of energy into him. He almost swayed into it, and I was briefly afraid I'd overdone it. But he just licked his lips and smiled again.

His eyes grew even darker. "Shall we go upstairs?"

My heart hammered in my throat. This was it. The moment I had to exert every ounce of persuasion I had over him.

"No," I whispered, stepping close to him, so our bodies were almost touching. "Here."

His eyebrow twitched. "Anyone could walk in, doll."

"Exactly," I breathed, closing the tiny gap between us. Right away, I could feel his arousal pressing against me. Oh, yes. The plan was going swimmingly.

With sudden movement, he set his drink down on the cart and pulled me into a bruising kiss.

I dropped my own glass, hearing it shatter on the marble floor, as little splashes of spilled brandy landed on my legs. Bastian didn't seem to notice or care. His hands gripped my waist, and in spite of myself, I thought of Dante.

I remembered our encounter in the dream world, when I pulled him into my web. But just like our "practice" in the woods, it wasn't a one-sided thing, not like it's meant to be with a succubus. I was supposed to take what I needed from him and go. Instead, he took a part of me, too.

The connection grew stronger with every moment we spent together. And now, even though I was seducing another man, Dante was all I could think about. I blocked out reality just enough to remember the taste of his lips. Imagine that it was his strong tongue seeking entrance to my mouth. I slid my hands up Bastian's back, but it was Dante who groaned against my lips.

Finally, Bastian broke away. "Here?" he panted. "Are you sure?"

I really didn't expect him to be so hesitant, but the urgency of his erection throbbing against my thigh told me it wouldn't take any of my special powers to convince him.

"Please," I moaned as he ducked in to kiss and nibble at my neck. "Please, Bastian . . ."

With a growl, he grabbed the material of my dress on either side of the side-slit and ripped it.

Just as the threads gave way, there was a massive crashing noise from somewhere upstairs.

Instantly, Bastian pulled away, his eyes clearing of their lust. "What the hell was that?" he snapped, raking his hand through his hair as he made for the door. "Wait here, Ivy."

If Dante and his men were about to fight the mad scientist who created me, I was going to at least be an active participant. Even if I wasn't exactly sure whose side I was on.

Ripping off my shoes, I ran up the stairs after Bastian. He didn't seem to notice, taking them three at a time in a graceful leap I'd never seen before. There was shouting coming from down the hall, and he made a beeline for his bedroom.

Oh hell. We were totally fucked.

CHAPTER 17

DANTE

We were fucked.

Ignoring the throbbing in my spine, I stared at Brax. He stared back with unbridled panic in his eyes. We didn't have a Plan B for this.

Across the room, the bitch threw her head back and laughed. I still didn't know where she'd come from. She was dressed like a lawyer going to a business meeting, but her eyes glowed with purples and reds, the sure sign of black magic infused into her being. The invisible force field kept me and Brax flat on the floor, like a couple of damsels in distress.

In her hand, she clutched the little vial that held my blood. After all those years of blowing off Brax's fascination about the prophecy, I thought maybe he was onto something.

"Who the hell are you?" I huffed at her.

She laughed, deeper than any human voice could be. "Does it really matter, half-breed?"

"I mean, I have to admit I'm curious, too," Brax piped up.

Oh, my gods, shut up.

"Clearly, you know enough," she said. "You knew enough to hatch this plan with Ivy to steal back your blood. You know the power it holds. You know exactly what I'm planning to do with it. So why do the details matter? You're not going to live to see the sunrise."

Suddenly, the door slammed open. Bastian stormed in, a disheveled Ivy in tow.

Just when I thought it couldn't get any worse.

"Marla?" Bastian roared. "What in the seven hells are you doing?"

The bitch turned to him, her eyes storming. "Oh, for goodness sake. I was hoping I wouldn't have to kill you, too."

Bastian made a move toward her, but the force field knocked him to his knees. Coughing, he raised his head with effort. "I don't understand, Marla. Why are you doing this?"

"Because you're a small-minded idiot," she intoned. It somehow sounded like she spoke with two voices at once. "All wrapped up in your stupid experiments in your little lab. You don't comprehend what's at stake here. How long do you think these human vermin will let you keep playing your little games? Their time on this world is up. It's time for us to take what's ours."

"You're not making any sense," Bastian wheezed. He made an effort to crawl toward her, and her eyes flashed as she knocked him to the floor again with a flick of her head. I glanced over at Ivy, who met my gaze with resolve.

Intentionally or not, Bastian was distracting her. This could be our opportunity. We might still get out of this alive, if Ivy had any of her power left to use.

The animal side of my brain obsessed about whether Bastian had fucked her yet. Like it mattered, at a time like this. But it did matter. It mattered to me. Both sides of me.

She mattered to me.

So help me, but all I cared about was making sure she got out of here safely. After hundreds of years of this life, I was tired. But she had so much life left to live. So much fire.

I couldn't let her die here. Not like this.

Even if she ended up with that snake, Bastian, I had to give her a chance.

With a deep breath, I reached inside myself for powers I hadn't used in eons. I knew I had them. I'd touched on them briefly, just a little, to delve into Ivy's mind when she flexed her powers in the forest. I had to try to save her.

Dimly, I heard the argument between Bastian and Marla continue.

"Did you think it was just a coincidence how I convinced you to get his blood?" Marla was laughing. "I knew exactly what I needed, and I knew you were just crazy enough to get it for me."

"It was your idea," Bastian muttered. "All your idea. You told me he existed in the first place. I didn't even . . ." He stared up at her balefully. "You used me, Marla, all along. And here I thought you were my friend."

Her laugh grew even harsher. "So stupid. Still, after all this time, you never even suspected. You trust so easily, and I even told you that you'd live to regret it."

"I didn't think you were talking about yourself, you psychopath." Bastian pounded his fist on the floor.

"So, it's true, then?" Brax cut in helpfully. "All that stuff about the prophecy?"

A nerd to the very end. If I'd had the energy to roll my eyes, I would have.

"Ah, we have a scholar in the group." Marla turned her piercing gaze on him. "I knew you couldn't all be stupid. Yes, you've put the pieces together. Well done. It took Samil's necromancers a long time to translate and understand all the texts, but they finally realized what was being foretold. We're going to create the world-ending demon whose coming was written in the most ancient, most secret of books. It was only a few months ago that we stumbled across the original recipe, in a book bound with human skin, and written in a half-breed's blood."

"I mean, I just went to the library," Brax said. "But, hey, whatever works for you guys."

Marla threw her head back and laughed. "A jokester. I like this one. What's your name, child?"

"Brax," he said, his voice steady. "I have to say—Marla, was it? It's so nice to meet somebody who actually appreciates my line of study."

I was focusing all my energy on her. Marla hadn't caught on yet, distracted by Brax and Bastian. I looked over at Ivy and saw her furrowing her brow. She was exhausted. The sweat on her forehead, her low, shallow breaths, told me how little she had left to give.

Between the two of us, we might be able to bring down the force field just long enough to break free and overpower the sorceress.

Or, we might die trying.

My head ached from the effort, every muscle in my body tensed. It still wasn't enough. The force field didn't even waver, and Marla didn't react.

At this point, she almost had her back to us. She couldn't see what we were doing. Not that it mattered. We were trapped here on the floor.

Or were we?

Shaking, sweating, Ivy reached for me. She walked her fingers along the floor, inch by painful inch. I didn't understand what she was trying to do, but I knew I had to try to meet her halfway.

It hurt like hellfire, but I reached for her, too.

When our fingers finally touched, I knew it. The jolt of electricity. The power.

With a burst of energy, I entwined my fingers with hers. We both stared at Marla, focusing all our energies at the back of her head.

With an unearthly shriek, she whirled around.

A mistake.

With her forehead exposed to us, we were much more powerful. I realized the force field emanated from what you'd probably call her third eye, even though not visible. It was an apex of power.

And we were hitting it with everything we had.

CHAPTER 18

Ivy

From the stretch of my palm, a dark tendril of energy took shape. It slithered forward in its infancy before it rose from the floor like a deadly cobra.

The curl of my weapon seemed to hold more strength than I did as I continued to heave for breath upon the floor.

Marla never saw it coming.

My whip snapped toward her, the extension of my energy raging as it cracked loud like thunder. She stumbled backward, taking away my greatest advantage—surprise—and left me with something far better. A thin line of blood surfaced down the edge of her cheek and her eyes widened at the realization that I'd hit her.

Pure rage erupted into the air. The sound poured from her mouth with a screech as her eyes darkened to the shade of night. Their burning depths flickered strong as the spike of energy she suddenly manifested hurled toward us.

Dante wasn't thinking. He yanked my arm which sent me tumbling beneath him. I was crushed there, unable to flex even the length of my fingers as I heard his agonizing groan mingle with her sizzling energy.

Channeling all my strength, I shoved hard, sending Dante thudding to the floor beside me as I shoved myself to my knees. There was no time to tend to his wounds or make certain he still breathed—not with the very real threat of Marla striking us all down.

Bastian, though, had another idea. Weak and without force, he shoved himself to his feet and staggered forward. His fatigue made him look almost drunk as he swung for her, his curled fingers flying open in a snatch of her arm. Silently, I cursed the pilfered vial that refused to fall from her grip, but the moment her fiery eyes turned toward Bastian, there was no time to waste on hope.

Energy surged through me, flicking my whip forward with a vengeance. Though it fell short, the snap alone was enough to startle Marla and divide her attention between the two of us. Still, Bastian was closer.

She struck at him, the slam of her hand across his chest crackling with a torrent of energy that sent him flying backward. Like a rag doll, he tumbled across the floor. His head slamming down so solidly I hoped I wasn't the only one left.

If I was, I'd defend us to the death.

Partially reinvigorated by Dante's energy and stress-induced adrenaline, I pushed forward. I rose onto shaky feet and nearly growled at Marla. This bitch would pay for what she had done.

I charged for her, my speed pathetic and lethargic as she hurled jolt after jolt of magical energy my way. The closer I drew, the harder it became to avoid them entirely. I darted side to side, until one fateful throw had me dropping to the floor in a pile of limbs simply to avoid certain death.

It was there, as I directly faced her towering legs, that I struck.

She fumbled backward, a feral fury lighting her cat-like eyes. She knew she was too close as my whip reared back and cracked toward her.

Jolts of her own dark energy, thick and spherical with her last shreds of strength, careened toward me. Our weapons collided, and in a violent shock wave, they exploded.

I tumbled across the floor, my eyes slamming shut against the onslaught of dust and debris, and my arms shielding my head from the pelting sting of the magical eruption we'd created.

My head lifted in the settling grime, only to find my lungs heaving in deep coughs. She'd hurt me, if only a little, and as my eyes narrowed through the clouds, I knew I had one last chance to get her—or we were all screwed.

Our eyes met, and in unison, our attentions dragged to where the vial had slipped from her grip, resting on the floor partway between us.

I flung myself toward it, every fiber of my muscles crying out in agony as I reached for the vial.

"Ivy, get down!"

The urgency in Dante's voice had me skidding, chest down, across the floor. I glanced over my shoulder at the exact moment his crossbow clicked loudly in its release.

I held my breath, certain this would be it.

The bolt soared toward Marla, but before it could hit its mark, her human form disappeared.

A screeching raven took her place, its hurried lift leaving not a single feather to be marred by Dante's well-placed shot.

I scrambled forward, but I was too late.

In her sharpened talons, Marla snatched up the vial and soared for a tiny opening in the nearest window. Though Dante had reloaded, the next sail of his bolt thudded into the window's sill just as the raven flew free.

For a moment, the room was silent.

"Well, shit," Brax said.

Bastian turned to stare at the three of us before focusing his eyes on Brax. "Do you care to explain to me what in the hell just happened?"

"There's this prophecy," Brax said, "about the end of the world."

"Yes, I gathered that much," Bastian straightened the collar of his shirt. "I meant, do you care to explain what you're doing in my house? In my bedroom?"

"You stole my blood," Dante said.

We might have been somewhat united in our struggle against Marla, but he wasn't disposed to be friendly toward him.

"I wanted it back."

"Yes, well. Sorry about that. I have no interest in ending this world. In fact, I rather like it." He glanced to me. "I suppose you're a part of this, too?"

"No," Dante said quickly, gripping my arm. "I kidnapped her sisters to get her to help me. It's not her fault. She was just doing what she had to do."

"Or course," Bastian said, his eyes drifting from one to the other of us, reading more than Dante or I probably wanted him to know. His gaze softened a little. "Of course," he said again. "My Ivy would never willingly betray me like that. Not unless she had to."

My Ivy. Dante's grip on my arm flashed hot and tightened.

"I don't think you all understand the implications of this," Bastian huffed, brushing some imaginary crap off his tailored jacket. "Samil is . . . well. Let's just say, I knew him long ago. Even when he was a young sorcerer, he had dark ambitions. Self-destructive, even. We were partners in crime for a while, but we parted ways when it became obvious we had different goals. He was willing to cut a swathe of destruction in his path if it got him what he wanted. He didn't care about the consequences. I can only assume, in the passing decades, he's gotten worse. I haven't heard of him in years. In this case, no news is decidedly not good news."

"Shit." Brax whistled. "So, what now?"

Bastian exhaled heavily. "Well, I guess that depends. If you're all willing, we might be temporary allies in the name of saving this world we all enjoy living in . . . I assume."

Dante didn't answer. He watched Bastian with a predator's gaze.

"We're likely the only ones who know what Samil has planned," Bastian went on. "That gives us a head start."

"How do we know you're telling the truth about this?" Dante demanded. "You could be leading us all into a death trap."

Brax stood up and advanced toward Bastian. "Nice to meet you. I'm Brax."

"I gathered that." Bastian extended a hand, smiling amusedly. "I'm guessing you're about to read my recent memories, correct?"

"You got it!" Brax said cheerfully. "Just hang tight for a second; it's only awkward if we make eye contact while we're holding hands." He nodded silently for a few seconds, and then pulled his hand away. "He's not lying. He didn't know anything about this until just now."

"So?" Bastian's eyes roved the room. "Dante, I assume you have some cohorts to recruit into this. I'll bring in all the allies I can trust. Brax can probably help with double-checking that. We need to determine where she went and stop this ritual before it starts."

I cleared my throat. Every head in the room turned to look at me.

"And what if we're too late?" I asked.

Bastian sighed. "Let's cross that bridge when we come to it."

Dante shook his head. "Hold up. I haven't agreed to anything. There is no 'we.'"

"This is no time for petty rivalries," Bastian replied firmly. "We stop this, or we die trying. There are simply no other options. I'm not going to sit and wait for the Apocalypse to come. Besides, I think it's pretty clear Ivy has already made her choice."

There was a hint of sadness in his eyes and a totally unexpected wave of guilt hit me. I scrambled to my feet. I wasn't going to deny it, Bastian was right. I had chosen—and it wasn't him, but he also still had a power over me. One I couldn't deny. We had to come to some new arrangement. I was about to speak, but Bastian held up a hand to silence me.

He glanced at Dante and Brax "Could both of you give me a moment with her?" I looked up to Dante and nodded, trying to say everything I hadn't in one look. I didn't want Bastian, I wanted him. Dante. Even after all of this.

"Come on," Dante grunted, going for the door. "Let's go take care of some unfinished business."

CHAPTER 19

Ivy

My head was still spinning with exhaustion. I couldn't process everything I'd learned in the past half hour, and the new, tentative alliance between the two men in my life was just as baffling as it was necessary.

Bastian advanced, and at first, I cringed. I knew what I deserved. Even if Dante had forced my hand, I chose to use the powers Bastian had given me against him.

But Bastian looked tired. As tired as I was.

"I'm not angry, pet," he said, sighing. "As much as I wish I could be. But I saw what you can do. More importantly, I saw what you can do when you join forces with him. I'd be foolish to ignore that. Foolish, even for me."

I swallowed hard, shaking my head. "You're . . . you're not an idiot. I mean, I guess Marla knows better than me, but—"

He laughed. "I can be, at times."

"I know what you wanted," I told him, meeting his gaze with honesty for the first time in my life. Shit, it was weird to acknowledge the elephant in the room. "I know you wanted to really own me, every part of me. I'm sorry I couldn't give you all of me."

"Don't apologize," he said softly. "It was stupid of me to believe you'd fall in love with your creator. I gave you a gift, but it was also a curse. I just hoped you'd come to overlook it. But it was idiotic of me to ever vie for your heart. I've always been more in love with my work than I could ever be with another soul, no matter how beautiful. I can't control who you love. If you ever change your mind, then so be it. But I can't force you. And I wouldn't, even if I could."

Strangely, I believed him. I sensed he was being completely genuine —maybe for the first time in his life.

"I still feel bad," I admitted. "I mean . . . if you want to trade in the. . . *date* I owed you for something else?"

He cut me off, laughing. "No trades necessary. If you want me, you can have me. The offer stands, no matter what. But not because you feel obligated. Give me some credit, doll."

I didn't know what to say. I guess I never had with him. But today, of all days, I was grateful for his kindness. Even if it was conditional, even if he was only working his own agenda, like he was apt to do. At least he cared.

"Thank you," I told him. And I meant it.

I was running. But for once in my life, I wasn't running from something, but after *someone*. I'd lived all my life building up walls and pushing people away. The only space I'd ever had left in my heart was for my sister's. But now. . . now Dante had changed all that.

When I got out to the steps, fat drops of rain splattered on my heated skin. I kept running, praying my bare feet wouldn't slip on the wet stone.

Dante and Brax were still in the gravel driveway, heads close together, talking quietly but animatedly. They both looked up, startled, when I approached.

"I thought . . ." Dante started.

"It was a quick conversation," I said before he could continue. "I want to help him, Dante. Are you coming with us?"

He hesitated. "They took my blood," he said at last, gruffly. "Forget 'em. I'm taking it back."

I grinned. I couldn't help myself.

The three of us trekked to the motorcycles. I guessed Dante had already dismissed the rest of his men, but I only concentrated on his proximity, the heady memory of what it had been like when our fingers had laced together. It was like the most potent drug in the world. Together, we were a thousand times more powerful than we could ever be alone.

I didn't know what we were going to face when we tracked down Marla and this Samil Bastian seemed to know a little too well. But whatever it was, I was excited. Strangely thrilled. Because, between the two of us, I knew we could accomplish the unbelievable.

When we reached the clearing with the bikes, Brax coughed nonchalantly. "I'll, uh, I'll go get the girls," he said. "Take them home. If that's all right with y'all."

Dante jerked his head "Thanks," he said. "Appreciate it."

I knew I should go with Brax, see my sisters safely home. But I couldn't leave Dante's side.

Once Brax's bike peeled away, I turned to the hulk of a man who stood there silent by my side. "So, I . . ."

He didn't give me a chance to finish before he kissed me like I already belonged to him, body and soul. He kissed me like we'd already been lovers.

In a way, I supposed we were.

The connection we shared was more intimate than sex. We'd peered into the dark corners of each other's souls and found something there to love. That darkness that scared others only pulled us together, united us.

We kissed like two people the cosmos had destined to be together. We kissed like every star-crossed couple from every story ever told since the beginning of time.

But most importantly, we kissed like Ivy and Dante.

We were just us.

Which was all we needed to be.

Our hands fumbled with each other's clothes, Dante's fingers grasping desperately at my breasts, palming and caressing them roughly through the delicate silk of my dress. I moaned into his mouth, biting gently at his lip.

With a groan, he grabbed me by the hips and lifted me up onto the seat of his bike. I spread my thighs as he pushed the material of my dress out of the way to roughly cup me through my panties. He growled softly as the heat of my arousal met his questing fingers.

"Who else has been here tonight?" he panted into my ear as I nuzzled his neck.

"No one," I gasped. "Only you."

"And why is that, gorgeous?"

"Because it's yours."

It was like a script we'd rehearsed a thousand times. Both of us knew our parts so naturally, like we were meant to be.

Ripping the delicate material aside, he situated himself between my aching thighs. "Yes?" he whispered into my mouth.

"Yes," I breathed.

And then, we were one.

Time stopped while we drank each other in, my fingers raking down his back, my cries swallowed in the heat of his mouth. When I reached my peak, my whole body shook and arched with pleasure. He soon followed.

In the silence afterward, punctuated only by our ragged breathing, I heard the soft chirping in the woods around us. The warm night air caressed us, like nature itself knew what we were supposed to be.

Together.

Always.

Two fucked up individuals made into one perfect fucking couple—and I wouldn't have it any other way.

EPILOGUE

Ivy

"Are you sure about this?" Brax asked yet again.

"I've never been less sure about anything in my life," Lila said, her mouth a thin line. "But it doesn't sound like we have much of a choice."

Bastian appeared around the corner of the yard, two of his guards following with an arsenal in tow. "Lila, I told you. The intel is good. But if you want to stay and hold down the fort."

She shook her head firmly. "No. If Violet goes, I go. I'm not letting her risk her life without me there."

I had never seen this side of her before, this momma-bear mentality. I supposed I liked it, strange as it was.

The past few days had gone by in a whirlwind of preparation, training, and tearful explanations and goodbyes. Bastian had honored our agreement and released Jade and Violet from the blood bond. But what happened next, had been a total shock: Bastian offered me an out. A real, *legitimate* out.

No longer would I be bound to servitude or tied to his magical will. But seeing as he couldn't lose his entire 'team,' he Instead offered another arrangement. One that allowed me the freedom I desired. It only cost me five years of favors and not of the sexual kind. Dante made certain of that. In exchange, he'd teach me how to harness my powers and master them.

Now, for the first time in our lives, my sisters and I were splitting up.

To say I was uneasy about the prospect would be an understatement, but I knew that the alternative to sitting back and letting things 'work themselves out' wasn't a real option.

Dante and I were headed South, following a lead we had on a Samil, where Violet, Brax and Lila and Bastian headed East after Marla. Jade stayed behind, with a great deal of protest, under the protection of some of Bastian's most trustworthy guards and Dante's men, Blaze and Kylo.

We had assembled a core team, and then a convoy around us, like we were going to war.

In a way, we were.

I reached out and grasped Dante's hand. He didn't look at me, but he didn't have to. I knew he smiled when his fingers laced with mine.

"Right, then," Brax said, shoving one more pile of books into the backseat of a dark-tinted van. "Let's all get to work, shall we?"

The end . . . *for now.*

CURSED MOONS & ANCIENT RUNES
SHADOW CREATURES BOOK TWO - COMING 2019!

KEEP READING FOR THE FIRST CHAPTER OF CURSE OF IRON, THE
HALFBLOOD HUNTRESS CHRONICLES, BOOK 1!

HALF-BLOOD
HUNTRESS CHRONICLES

CURSE
OF
IRON

USA TODAY BESTSELLING AUTHORS
MIERS & KNOX

THE LEGEND

"Tiocfaidh an leathling chun críche do réimeas, ag caitheamh draíocht Gaia ó lámh seanóirí wicca, agus coróin na Fae a athnuachan"

"The halfling will come to end your reign, tearing Gaia's magic from the hands of the elders of wicca, and restoring the crown of the Fae..."

The child was born on the tenth day of the tenth month, one hundred years after Morgana cursed her own kind to dwindle in power until the great coven was no more. Her mother was a high priestess of Gaia, her father the heir apparent to the throne of the Seelie Fae, the light court of Fairy.

But the priestess could not survive the hate and fear, and somehow, the strong, vibrant witch died during childbirth. The Fae king was fading, his son poised to take the throne. His grief knew no release, but he had too many hidden enemies to allow them to know his daughter. He left her with the witches—to keep her safe from harm—and left fairies among the humans to keep watch over her until the time came when she would be strong enough to join him, or his throne was secure.

CHAPTER 1

THE FIRST THING I noticed when I jerked awake was my mouth tasted like sawdust and beer.

The second was the weight of another body beside me.

I must have drank more than I thought.

I didn't remember bringing a guy home and considering how long it had been I could've used the recollection of a good time. I swallowed trying to work up some moisture into my mouth, and inched closer to the edge of the bed, and reached for the light.

The form next to me was cool when my toes brushed against him and too still, making my heart pound excitedly. I turned on the bedside lamp and eased out of bed to look down at the naked man I'd woken up next to, his eyes wide and staring, already clouded by death.

It took a second to register his face, already twisted into his death mask.

Gideon Masters.

Gideon Masters, the baddest Alpha on this side of the continent is in my bed—and he's fucking dead. What in the fresh fuck is happening? Is this a nightmare?

I slammed my fist into the wall, sucking in air at the bruising pain in my knuckles. I backed away from the bed, revulsion twisting my stomach. *Holy shit, holy shit, holy shit,* my brain played the words on repeat like one of the old vinyl records my boss liked to play in the office. Gideon's lifeless eyes continued to stare at the ceiling, ensuring no matter what else, I wouldn't sleep there restfully, ever again.

He was naked from the waist up, revealing dark chest hair and fine cut abs. The blankets were pulled back enough to make my stomach lurch again at the realization he was definitely not wearing anything underneath, either. His skin had already begun to look waxy, even in the half light of the reading lamp, and my hand searched automatically for the wall switch before I stopped myself.

"You don't need a better look, stupid," I glanced at the window-shade, drawn, no sign it had been opened. "How the hell did you get in here?" I glanced around, looking for some clue to jog my memory, or explain how I'd woken up in a nightmare worse than any I'd had while sleeping. I tugged my long tee down over my legs, grateful I hadn't been nude next to him, cuddled skin to skin with death.

"Okay, stop freaking out and call someone," I glanced around for my phone. The charging stand next to the bed was empty, and my bag was nowhere in sight.

I backed toward the door, pushing the disgust and fear back, examining the bedroom as best I could. There was no blood on the bed and no sign of a struggle of any kind. Maybe he had a bad heart...or was sick...*or was poisoned by Aunt Portia and left here as a warning.*

I shuddered at the thought as my fingers found the doorknob behind me and I slipped out of the bedroom. With the horror hidden safely behind my door, I glanced around the living area of my apartment. If the body in my bed hadn't put itself there, I might not be alone. I dropped into a crouch behind the armchair and moved in a crab-like walk, visually clearing the living room, dining room, and kitchen, before I jumped up and raced to the denim satchel I used as a purse.

Grabbing my phone out of the bag, I ducked behind the island and started to dial, my eyes constantly glancing between the closed guest bathroom and the hallway which led to the two bedrooms. *Orson, pick up, pick up, pick up,* I begged silently as I listened to the trilling ring on the other end.

"What the hell, girl?" Orson growled from the speaker, but I didn't have a chance to answer him.

"Police! Open up!" The shout came from the hall. A moment later, my door crashed open, and I screamed, dropping my phone.

"Show your hands!" In seconds I was on my face against the cool wooden floor, my arms wrenched painfully behind my back as cops swarmed my apartment. I froze as a paralyzing spell landed on me.

"Watch out, she's a hexer," one barked, and they all backed away from me. Lying flat with my cheek pressed into the floor, I stared at the dust bunnies under my couch, the voices around me strangely muffled from my vantage point.

The witch-detective who had paralyzed me kneeled at my side, checking I was incapacitated before she gave the others permission to yank me to my feet. If they'd bothered to ask, I would've told them I was happy to comply, but they probably wouldn't have believed me anyway.

As her lips moved, my mind cleared enough to realize my rights were being read to me. I nodded my understanding because the spell wouldn't let me speak. It wasn't quite constitutional, but I worked with law enforcement every day. I knew how much harder the job had been for the last century, as magical beings stopped hiding in the shadows and entered mainstream society.

Two more cops appeared from my bedroom, calling the detective back with them, and my body finally rebelled, the knowledge of what I knew resided there, forcing bile into my still sealed mouth. I gagged on the vomit, choking, until the cop holding me upright yelled for the detective and she ran in, casting as soon as she saw what was happening.

They bent me over and she turned my head to one side as I spit and dragged a deep breath down my stomach acid scorched throat into my burning lungs. I managed to whisper, "Thank you," leaning into her as if she wasn't the person about to end my life as I knew it, my legs weak and trembling. The police held almost all my body weight. "I don't understand what's happening," I added, but silenced myself before she could decide to renew the spell.

"You're okay," she murmured, not quite sympathetic, but without accusation. "Just breathe." She tipped my chin up so I was forced to meet her eyes. They were the color of chocolate, and it made me think of how good chocolate would feel on my stinging throat. "You must be powerful, to take down someone so big."

I shook my head. "Not really. Besides, do you see any vines climbing my walls? My magic is growing things. New life, not death." The absence of magic had been one of the first things I'd noticed when the initial shock was over. "How did he die?"

The other officer jerked my arm hard enough to make my shoulder pop. "Like you don't know," he snarled and I dropped my eyes, holding my body still so he wouldn't yank on me again.

"Enough, Jones. You start knocking on doors. Sam and I will secure her in our vehicle."

"Yes ma'am, Detective."

I tried not to show my relief, even though she wasn't giving me special treatment. The paranormal division of the Oakland PD employed witches, reluctantly, to keep supernaturals under control when we were arrested. It came with certain benefits, like a fast track to promotions. Usually, I was all for better representation for my kind in the police department. It had saved a lot of magical lives when cops stopped shooting first under the assumption we were all immortal.

I'm half Fae and I could be hard to kill. But I wasn't about to start testing the theory, not when the other half was almost human-weak and just as slow to heal. The detective called out to her partner and the asshole on my left was replaced by a giant. He wasn't a literal giant, but he was huge compared to my five-foot-three inches.

"You okay there?" he asked, sincere concern radiating from him. "Tracy, was this self-defense?"

Detective Mills sighed, and I felt her shrug. "I dunno, Sam. There's no sign of a struggle, but he's awfully young-looking for a heart-attack."

"He's the alpha," I blurted, my usual helpful self being anything but as they walked me to their magically protected car. Steel and machines are difficult to enchant, their components being the literal antithesis of magic. All the growing pains resulting from our people coming out of hiding is why witch-detectives were so valuable, they've got to be the best to maintain control in magical situations.

"Fuck." The giant tightened his hold as he guided me down the narrow flight of stairs to the foyer. They had their routine down; him handling me and the doors, leaving her hands free to cast if necessary. If I had been stupid enough to try to escape.

"Look. I didn't do anything to him…to the man in my room," I began again as the male detective loomed over me, buckling me into my seat. I wasn't cuffed, the detective's spell was enough to control me even inside the car. "I only know him because he's like, famous around here."

The giant sighed. "Did they read her her rights?" I couldn't hear the reply, but he stuck his head in the window after shutting the door on me. "You need to stop talking until you get to the station, okay?"

I nodded, but I couldn't help myself. "But I work for Tell's Bail Bonds." I was horrified to find myself sniffling like our clients so often did. "I wouldn't break the law…"

But he had already vanished from view, and I was left to shake and cry in the back of the paranormal squad car as the crowd of onlookers around me grew.

CONTINUE READING MORGANA'S STORY IN CURSE OF IRON HERE!

DEAR READER,

Thank you so much for taking the time to read Gravestones & Wicked Bones. We hope you enjoyed reading about Morgan!

The next book in the Shadow Creatures series will be out in 2019! We can't wait to share the next part of the series with you!

If you enjoyed Gravestones & Wicked Bones, please consider leaving a review on Amazon or Goodreads. We love any and all feedback and every review counts!

If you'd like to be notified of upcoming releases, giveaways, and more, sign up for our newsletter!

Stay Wicked,
    Graceley & Dee

ALSO BY GRACELEY KNOX & D.D. MIERS

1. *Dark Summoner*

2. *Dark Illusions*

3. *Dark Secrets* (Coming Soon!)

4. *Dark Destiny* (Coming Soon!)

The Supernaturals of Los Melas

1. *Gretel: Witch Hunter*

Standalones:

City of Shadows: The Dark Fae Hollows

Wicked: The Isa Fae

Slayer in Lace

ABOUT THE AUTHORS

USA Today bestselling authors, Graceley Knox and D.D. Miers may be long-lost sisters, but their moms continue to deny it. They are most definitely the co-writers of the Kresova Vampire Harem series, as well as a multitude of other upcoming projects they can't wait to share with readers.

Together they tend to share the same brain, finish each other's thoughts, laugh way too hard at inappropriate comments, drink enough coffee to qualify for an intervention, and talk about their fur babies. When they're not chatting, which is always, they can be found all over social media hanging out with their author friends and readers!

Visit them at www.knoxandmiers.com
Sign up for their Newsletter here!